WADE

Douglas Gowland

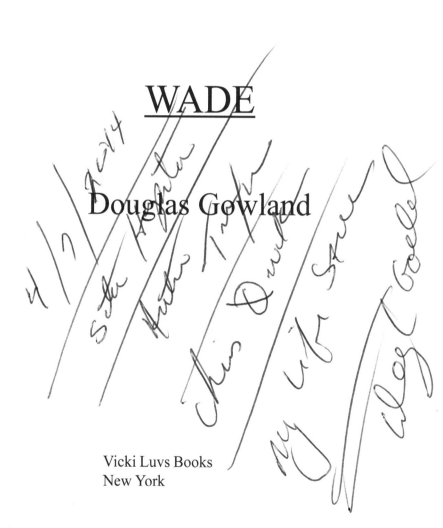

Vicki Luvs Books
New York

First Edition, September, 2003

 Published in the United States of America by Vicki Luvs Books, New York

Library of Congress Control Number 2003096155
ISBN 0-9729906-0-7

Manufactured in the United States of America

PUBLISHER'S NOTE
This is a work of fiction. Names, characters, places and incidents either are the product of the author's imagination or are used fictitously, and any resemblance to actual persons, living or dead, business establishments, events or locales is entirely coincidental.

To "Doc" & Mrs. Wideman

To Walter & Elena Chapin

With Love

DG
NYC

CHAPTER ONE

One heart—one soul—one dream!

They say you got to get a good job. Father said ... work hard. Mother said ... get a good girl.

They needle. They begin when you're young. I know. I was there.

If it was the Chinese water torture, your forehead against the drips, you could look up and see the water. But the needling comes at all angles. All times. All degrees. They brainwash.

"What are you gonna do when you grow up?"

For them, conception was the result of

me. Two young bodies seeking warmth on a cold February night. In a one-bedroom bungalow, they found tenderness and love in a legal age of marriage. Rent, thirty-five dollars a month.

Unlike today, when rent is higher and you don't have to be legal to conceive. Their dreams were the same as others. A job. A family. And that ultimate dream, a two bedroom home in Florida.

The writer added a period to his statement and reread the page. He closed the book and stuffed it into his athletic bag at his side. As he glanced at the clock in the lobby, he heard the elevator "ding" as it arrived. To the clock, eleven forty-seven. Nobody on the elevator. He looked through the double glass doors into the street ... no Junior.

"Junior. Junior, of all days to be late, today is not the day. Junior, please." The speaker turned toward the elevator bank again with the second ding.

A small dapper Englishman with a Savoy Row bowler and gold-topped cane appeared. He could have been six foot in his prime, but a gentle age reduced him to five ten. He walked briskly through the door that was opened for him as he expected.

"Good afternoon, Master Wade," with an English clip.

"Noon, sir. Another lovely spring day in the Village,

sir." As Wade held the door, he checked his watch. It was only 11:55, but he had set his watch five minutes fast. That agreed with Mister Acton-Stone who also checked his watch.

Wade made sure he opened the right-hand door as Mister Acton-Stone left the building and the left-hand door when coming home.

"Master Wade," he would intone, as if he had a cold all year round, "the right-hand door. The civilized world uses the right-hand door. The world revolves to the right." A quick sniffle to those who use the left-hand door.

"You use the right door? Master Wade?"

Wade pondered two things. One, being called "master" at the age of thirty-two. And two, that being smart to Mister Acton-Stone would violate the boss' Rule Number 1 … "To be rude is to be a goner."

"Yes sir. I am the doorman," Wade answered.

"That's a good lad." Mr. Acton-Stone waited while Wade opened the second door.

By Wade's watch, it was twelve-five. By the Seth Thomas in the lobby, it was noon. Junior was still late. Five minutes ... late is late. Wade took a sip of coffee from his mug and thought about what his life had become … cold coffee.

He took a fresh page from his notebook and made a list:

1. Rik.

2. Rikki.
3. Rikki-tikki.
4. Laundry.
5. Vacuum.
6. Rent $225.
7. Telephone $35.
8. Soup.
9. Shampoo.
10. TP.
11. Wrap pennies.
12. Apples.
13. Stop thinking about her … Stop thinking about ... Stop thinking … Stop ...

My heart feels as if ... it is pumping peanut butter.

Wade remembered the first time he met his boss Henry, the building manager. If Wade wanted the job, it was his. But Henry had a couple of Cutty Sarks on the rocks. Wade only smiled.

Henry was a good customer, and every Friday, promptly at four bells, Henry would have three Cutty Sarks and Wade would offer one on the house. To dilute the scotch, Henry would bring his own can of Spanish peanuts. The bar served goldfish snacks, for those who drank too much and turned their stomachs into aquariums.

Henry would talk about his "building." Buildings didn't go by the fancy names developers had christened them, but by the addresses. And "66" was a modern day phallus, among the century-old, five-story townhouses, on the prettiest street in the Village.

At one end of the street, number "One" was a renovated, upscale building, featuring track lighting, sunken kitchens and tasteless art in the hallways. The apartments were always empty because the owners were always out of the country. On the ground floor, a new restaurant opened every six months. This month it featured Day-Glo Mexican drinks and a bouncer who wore black and admitted you, if you drove a German car.

At the other end of the street, number "120" was the last stop in a fall from grace — a flophouse for unemployed stevedores and dockworkers. It offered a view of their former place of employment and the rats that scurried along the dock, competing with them for life. At both ends of the street, the ships of opportunity sailed into view and are gone forever.

But number "66" housed those who had caught the right ship at the right pier and Henry was the building manager. A former Navy man.

"Stand around. Any shift you want. All the coffee you can drink. Hold the door. Take packages. Mostly laundry."

Henry swirled the ice in his glass, and Wade topped the drink with a swift move of the bottle. "You don't have to mop. That ain't so bad." Henry popped a peanut into his mouth, confident that a deal was made.

He unhitched the giant key ring on his belt, the symbol of his authority and with the fist covering the ring on the bar, he wrapped his calloused hand around the rocks glass.

"I got a job," answered Wade, shrugging his shoulders.

Wade did have a job, and the record showed that it was Wade's forty-third job after college. But Wade didn't keep count. A job is a job, some more fun than others. All started with the excitement and thrill, ended with the boredom of routine and then the urge to leave. The beauty of bartending was that you ate in the restaurant, every night was a party and tips.

For three years, Wade worked nights at the Rusty Anchor and held different jobs during the day, liquor store, sporting goods store and the clothing store. Earlier, when his degree had a look and feel as crisp as his neckties, corporate life had appealed to him. Now his degree was turning to parchment as mottled as those ties. Wade tried graduate school, but it tried him.

Europe appealed to him. Until he went there. The trip he dreamed about for years only lasted six weeks. He planned to stay a year, grow his hair long and cultivate a beard, eat French cuisine, sit in a cafe, drink aperitifs. To roam the streets of Paris with grand thoughts of life and morality. To be Paris.

But after six weeks, a hot shower, a cold beer and a baseball game were the only thoughts on his mind. A cute American girl, with a smile would be his new morality. French women never smile at anyone who talks of Sartre and has a scraggly beard.

He liked Americans and he liked America.

Wade returned to his hometown and a succession of jobs. Then his father stated that Wade had worked for everyone in town. So he left.

The city appealed to him. There were no other frontiers for him to conquer. He didn't have a spaceship. He didn't have a submarine. He didn't seek new horizons, but new people. People who laugh, think, create, love. People who question and make things happen. That was his journey.

The Rusty Anchor was a stop on a pub crawl, after a ball game. The name of the bar described the bar perfectly. It had been there since the Civil War, a little rust, a little secure spot. A bulletin board had a weathered three-by-five card that stated, "If you have a college degree and you're broke, see the manager." Wade was hired and made head bartender by staying sober.

Wade ran the bar, maintained the inventory, made out work schedules, and deposited the receipts in the safe. Angela, the bookkeeper, put the cash in the bank.

Wade liked the job and the customers came from the neighborhood. Every night Wade left a note for Angela. To aid in his reporting, Wade began keeping a notebook in his athletic bag. He kept notations and lists, who wanted nights off, employees phone numbers, inventory. As time went by Wade began to write notes to himself, a joke, a string of words that sounded good, odd bits of information and then, the book became a part of him.

Wade topped off Henry's scotch and went down to the other end of the bar where the waitresses stood at the service station. Jenny wanted a beer for a customer, but Mary wanted a shoulder rub and turned around for a "quickie."

"I'm next," said Jenny, as she left with the beer.

The relationship between the waitresses and the bartender is built on economics and good feelings. If your waitress is in a foul mood, you have a long night and poor "tip backs." So Wade rubbed her shoulders until she purred. Waitresses are athletes. They do five miles a night, lift ten times their weight, while dodging doors, customers, and drunks like any halfback.

"Thanks, Wade." Mary returned in kind a compliment to build her relationship for the evening. "You can rub my body anytime." She winked and left.

"Promises, promises," Wade added.

Wade returned down the bar to Henry, but he was gone. He removed the napkin and cleaned the glass and nibbled on the few remaining peanuts in the blue can. Wade opened his notebook and wrote.

"How can I sleep, Mommy? The circus parade is tomorrow. Elephants, horses, tigers, monkeys, clowns, lions, and more clowns," he said, standing beside the bed in his pajamas.

"If you don't sleep, tomorrow will never come. There will be no parade," Mommy said. And, as if by magic, his eyes squinched shut and the "Sandman of Sleep" came to his bedroom.

Tomorrow did come, not soon enough for an eight-year-old. He got out of bed and padded to the bathroom to brush his teeth. But sleepy eyes did not see what Mommy spotted immediately. Measles.

His sister saw the parade and saw Mister Peanut, who gave her a pink Mister Peanut Bank. He cried and wished he could give his sister the measles.

Wade closed his notebook and gave Jenny the peanut can. She placed it in the waitress station and pulled out a handful of pennies from her apron and put them in the can.

"Have you ever had the measles?" asked Wade as he began to stare at imaginary spots on her face.

"No." She pulled out her makeup mirror. But the mirror was too small and she rushed to the ladies' room.

Bartending shifts start at five, but Wade liked to get to

work at four, talk to the day- bartender, and prepare for his night shift. Jay, the day bartender, was sitting customer side of the bar with a cigarette and an airplane magazine. He was a tall, lean man. His balding pate and wire glasses made him look thinner because his nose was long and his nostrils kicked up. He was probably a stork in an earlier life.

Jay smiled at everyone and had been at the Rusty Anchor longer than anyone. Two years ago, Jay talked about flying lessons. After a moment of "how are you doing?", Jay pulled out sheets of graph paper with designs and spread them across the bar.

"This is the baby I been talking about." Jay began a discourse on the aerodynamics of adding a strut here and a wing support. It was rocket science to Wade. This was not the sketching by a bored sophomore in biology class, with little bombs being dropped on the high school, but serious point by point designs.

"A motorized pterodactyl ... eighty foot, wingspan, cockpit, wheels, instead of legs." Jay pointed to the sketch.

"The evolution of flight at its purest form, before man's input. Simple flying."

"Of course." Wade sipped his coffee and looked back at Jay and thought he wanted to fly a Piper Cub.

"I'm going to build it myself." Jay laid his pencil down and looked at Wade.

"Good." Wade got up and went behind the bar. How

does one encourage a friend, but not become Fool's partner?

"It may work," Wade finally said.

"It will fly." Jay stood up from his stool.

Wade mentioned pterodactyls needed great heights to soar off.

"Exactly my reasoning. Speed has no limits, but the mark of great flyers is 'how' he flies. This is pure flying. Simplest form. I plan to fly off my apartment building and soar into aviation history."

Wade knew he had said the wrong thing. His left-handed encouragement of how to be a dinosaur could lead to his friends extinction.

Jay folded his graphs and grabbed his coat.

"I knew I could count on you, Wade."

The evening shift employees watched "M*A*S*H" before coming to work. It was a written rule somewhere, and Wade climbed up on the stool and powered the set above the back bar. His work would keep him busy, thus the television was a big radio and if he heard something funny he would turn to watch.

Restaurant employees are always late because they don't leave the house until the show ends. Then at work they re-enact each scene and discuss the message. The message was the undertone.

Queenie, the head waitress, thought the message was

the stars' way of putting across their point of view of the world. Wade understood, since his favorite show was Perry Mason. It was his belief that the actor told the audience who the killer was, by touching his face or tweaking his nose whenever he spoke to the killer. This was Wade's theory.

This was a M*A*S*H bar. Radar was loved by the girls. To listen to them, you would have thought they had already been intimate. Queenie liked Hawkeye, he had purpose. Queenie's purpose was money and getting as much as she could. She had worked her way up from busgirl to waitress to head waitress. She was exacting, concerning who worked what shift and their conduct to the customers. She was not above publicly letting an employee know her thoughts. But money had become her quest. When the girls talked about their boyfriends, Queenie only wanted to know if they had money. She judged men by the cost of their clothing.

"He's definitely a 50." She would say, meaning he pulled down $50,000 a year.

She had red hair down to her shoulders and that changed to orange when she was angry. "Orange hair, bartender beware."

Wade thought she was sharp but lacked education or marketable job skills other than those of a waitress.

"Good qualities for a wife." He would say and Queenie would smile.

But Queenie's pursuit altered her thinking as she sought

out counseling, self-help groups, socials and mixers, and video dating, through her new church group, the Visual Believers of Jeremiah. Wade suspected they were the "firewalkers" from a few years back, but Queenie said they were into water and ice.

"With bourbon." Wade suggested. Queenie failed to see the humor.

The shift started and he felt he was working in a fog, but shrugged it off. A couple of customers entered the bar and Wade winked to Queenie.

"Here comes a 75!" Wade pointed.

Queenie would rush to the door and greet the customer and judge him, feet first.

"Weejuns, $45, athletic socks, $1; Levis (pressed), how could he!, $29, button-down shirt, $42, Orlon sweater, $90, haircut, $30. Steel Rolex, $650, no wedding band. In advertising. Possible 48."

Queenie was looking for a 200, but it was the pursuit that kept her going.

Wade never pursued Queenie because he preferred to do the pursuing and refused to be judged by the cut of his denim.

The regulars of the bar came in. Barry Baseball sat at his usual spot. He had a newspaper from the Caribbean. Wade placed a beer in front of him.

"Yankees ... mumble, mumble something mumble ... They send these kids to winter ball and they need pitching." He was not happy. Barry had a real last name, but he earned his nickname. The girls agreed they were attracted to him because he was low key. He did not push.

"I have a date with Barry Baseball. Don't tell a soul or I'll puke in your icebox," Jenny stated proudly. Waitresses can be cruel.

A couple of Wall Street sharks came into the bar and ordered gin and tonics. Queenie's eyed widen. The Big Shark drank two drinks to Little Shark's one.

"You must be new here." The Big Shark had bags under his eyes.

"Yes, I am." Wade said, pausing for effect. "About three years."

Big Shark smiled and slid five dollars across the bar. "We're looking for some girls." Indicating the waitresses.

"They're all around. Whole world full of them." Wade slid the five back across the bar. The men downed their drinks and left. No tip.

"I don't go out with married guys." Queenie reminded the other girls.

"How did you know?" asked Mary Ann.

"They kept their left hand in the pocket."

Jimmy Grease came in and sat two stools down from Barry Baseball. His nickname was appropriate because his hands were fresh from the oil pan. When Wade put the beer mug down, Jimmy had to use both hands to pick it up because his hands were so slick.

“’Mary Ann, you went out with Jimmy Grease?” Jenny was incredulous.

“We only went to the beach, during the day.” Mary Ann revealed her secret, now eight months old, as if no crimes against humanity are committed in broad daylight.

“Mary, you’re a masochist.” Jenny left to deliver her drinks.

“What’s religion got to do with it?” Mary Ann looked at Wade and twitched her nose. Wade delivered another drink to Jimmy.

“Wade, you dork all these waitresses around here?” Jimmy finished his drink in a swallow. Barry Baseball stopped reading.

“Not me. Jimmy, never dance on the table where you eat.”

Barry snickered and returned to the box scores.

“I’m dead. I got laid off. My stroking days are over.” Jimmy put his head down. “You hear of anything, let me know. No money, no fun.”

Wade nodded and went back to the waitress station where Mary Ann and Jenny were talking.

“He talked about cars the whole time at the beach. He said how good it would be when we made love. It was our first date. I never took off my top and jeans. I said I was sunsick.

He would have grabbed me if he saw my two-piece." Mary Ann's lower lip protruded and her brow came below her bangs.

"The slime dog. Never go out with guys with thin noses. Didn't I tell you?" Jenny jerked her head toward Jimmy and took her tray away. Jenny would never compete with Socrates or Aristotle, but to Mary Ann pure wisdom flowed from her mouth.

Wade came back to Jimmy and Barry.

"Mechanics always work," said Barry. "Good ball player always finds a game."

"Don't know this time. Things are drying up in the shops. These foreign trucks are not like American trucks. American trucks break down. I got to change my ways. I got to get a new life."

"Good infielder goes from second to third, shortstop. No problem." Barry was reassuring.

"Shade tree mechanic can fix anything," said Wade. "Fix Toyotas."

"I like American. They look good. Drive good. I can put them back together. That's what I do." Jimmy knew his place. "I got to go back to the basics, save my money. No fun for awhile." Jimmy saw the future.

"No fastball too fast for a hitter." Barry finished his drink and wished Jimmy the best. Wade cleaned up the glass and napkin. Jimmy lowered his head as his two drinks in rapid succession took effect.

"I got-to ... I need someone to help me ... I got to change... I got nobody." Jimmy moaned.

"Jimmy, your life is about to change. Just keep your mouth shut." Wade flicked his nails on the bar and then went down to the waitress station and called Queenie over.

"Did you watch "M*A*S*H" today?" Wade asked. He put up a cranberry and soda for her. This was an offering. She took the drink and leaned on the bar.

"Radar adopted a rabbit," she replied.

"What did that symbolize?" Wade asked.

"Fertility. Radar hasn't had a girlfriend in a long time." She sipped on her drink.

"Oh, how about lost creatures. Wasn't it a hospital, the M*A*S*H unit? Radar isn't a doctor, but ... he can take care of something. He could take care of ... a rabbit." Wade had to reach for that one, since he was doing inventory and vaguely remembered the storyline.

"Yes, but rabbits symbolize sex." Queenie perked up.

"What are we? We're a M*A*S*H unit of sorts. Lost soldiers, wounded souls in a place to get well. I take care of those that I can take care of, and you take care of those you can heal." Wade dug in the ice for a minute to avoid her look.

"You're like Hotlips, always looking for that rich guy, but so far he hasn't come long ..." Wade was on thin ice. "You want to be swept away?" Wade looked at her.

"Yes." She sipped her drink.

"Hotlips is always finding guys that need her help, those that she can ... resurrect. Prince Charming doesn't have to be wearing a suit of shining armor, you know. He could be rather plain." Wade took a long drink and looked down to see if his plan was sticking. He crossed his fingers and closed the trap.

"Jimmy Grease sold his shop and is sitting on a cool ...." Wade shrugged his shoulders and quickly walked down the bar to Jimmy.

As he walked by Jimmy, he leaned over.

"Nobody. No customer, has dorked Queenie, that I know of." Wade walked off. That was a fib. A woman has to lead her own life.

Wade went back to the waitress station and looked at Queenie, who had a disgusted look on her face.

"Get him a shave, haircut. Get him out of those T-shirts and jeans. He doesn't know how to spend his money. Clean up his language, take him to church. None of the other girls would take him from you." Wade loved to play Cupid. What poetic justice, this union!

Queenie leaned over Wade's shoulder and peered at Jimmy who had his head down looking into his drink or his future. She tried to imagine him with a shave.

Wade pulled out the vodka bottle and hit her drink. She noticed the gesture and took a big gulp. Queenie walked around the bar to Jimmy and sat down.

The shift went a little easier for Wade after that. When he got home at 3:00 a.m., he opened a pint of orange juice and sat at his desk to write in his notebook.

"Look, Mommy."

The ten-year-old was wearing his pajamas bottoms and playing with his baseball mitt on top of the bed.

"This is how you stop a grounder." He dropped to one knee like a pro. His sister did the same on her bed. She didn't have a glove.

"The bunt." He stood and went into a bunt stance. His sister followed suit.

"The home run swing." He did his Mickey Mantle swing. Sister too. Mommy smiled.

"Rounding the bases." The boy began to trot in place on the bed. His sister mimicked him on the other twin bed.

"Watch me." Mommy watched. "First base." He turned in the same spot. "Second. One handed ..." He dropped one hand to his waist and continued to jog in place.

"Third base. No hands." He dropped the other hand and continued to jog.

"Home!" He plopped onto the pillows. His sister did likewise.

Mommy picked up her book to read a bedtime story.

"Mommy, can I play baseball this summer?" Sister asked from under the covers.

"She can't play baseball, Mommy. She's a girl," Brother said in distaste.

"I want to play too! Can I, Mommy?"

"Yes, dear, you can play. I did," Mommy said.

"You played baseball, Mommy?" His eyes bugged out.

"First base." Mommy said proudly.

First base was his position.

"I want to play first base like you, Mommy." Sister beamed.

Brother pulled the blankets up to his chin and lay shaking as Cinderella was read. His thoughts were not of a charming prince seeking out a beautiful princess, but thoughts worse than thc boogieman under the bed.

A girl standing on first base.

Dad should know about this.

When Wade awoke, a cinnamon biscuit was the taste he craved — not a danish, not a sweetroll or a muffin or a lemon twist, cookie or piece of toast. It could be round or flat. But it had to be cinnamon. He couldn't remember his mother making cinnamon biscuits, but she must have, since all mothers make biscuits. This was his morning quest, but there was not much time left in the a.m. A cup of coffee. A cinnamon biscuit, and the paper. What better way to spend a Saturday morning? He grabbed his ball cap and his jacket, but the cold hallway floor reminded him that shoes would help. He returned to his apartment and put on his sneakers. No socks.

As he put on his shoes Wade thought of a television star with blond hair and a jaw the shape of a ship's prow that needed barnacles scraped off. The television star was a new sensation because he didn't shave and didn't wear socks.

"Big deal." Wade giggled. Years ago, half the college students didn't wear socks with their penny loafers. Some didn't wear shoes. They pressed their futures with chants. "Hell, no, we won't go" and "Damn, damn, Vietnam" and were arrested by the bad guys. They had songs of protest and glory on their lips and nothing on their toes. Yet years later, this television star, hung his career on phrases like "You're mine, Jocko" and arrested all the bad guys, garnered all the sockless press.

He had nothing on his lips but his toes were sung to glory.

The fresh air bit into his lungs and cleaned out the gunk.

The bar was smoky and had a machine called a smoke-eater, but both the machine and his lungs got eaten. His legs were tight and the walk felt good. It was early fall becoming winter and the sky was battleship gray. His sweatpants matched the sky, but his mood was summer day. Life was good and would get better at the deli with its fogged over windows and steaming coffee and waiting cinnamon biscuits.

The deli man spoke no English. Wade wanted to say, "Good morning. How are you today? Could I have a cup of coffee and a cinnamon biscuit. I have the paper here." But the deli man spoke no known language represented at the United Nations or even encountered by the Starship Enterprise. Wade was reduced to quick eye contact and what passed for a grunt like "Koffybiskitpaper." Anything else and Wade would be standing there for an hour. Tourist were easy to spot enunciating each word and pointing to the salami and then in frustration shouting, "Ham and cheese on rye. Coke."

But the deli man spoke American dollar and could say, "dollar eighty-five" very distinctly while ringing up $1.00 on the cash register. That's how the deli worked.

With his breakfast in hand and newspaper, food for the mind and body, Wade started home. An elderly lady was picking up dog poop in front of the deli and an ambulance siren whooshed screaming by, he hardly noticed. He had lived here long enough that only a lack of noise could attract his attention. His block was very busy with traffic with a bus stop at the corner. The busses created loud rumblings and "bus farts" as they started their engines. His apartment was in the rear building, so it was quieter.

As he pushed his front door open at street level, Wade stopped and looked down. A crumpled five dollar bill lay at his feet, with the speed of a cat he swooped down in one motion stuffed it into his pocket. He stepped into the vestibule. Fumbling for his keys and smirking over his good fortune, Wade heard a haunting sound. A sound that inspired small town people to move, little boys to wander, little girls to dream of city lights, and grown men to weep for lost horizons. The sound people hear in the middle of hot summer nights as they lie in their beds. The wail that inspired musicians to write songs of love and sadness. The sound of a train whistle.

But this is the Village. Here there are no trains, no stations.

Wade stepped back into the street and tilted his head. Nothing. Shaking it off he stepped back into the doorway and put the key in the lock. There it was again, the low wail of a train in the distance. An image of the midnight train across the plains that led men to see the worlds and boys to become engineers, came to him, Wade listened for half a second and figured it was the pipes in the building. Mrs. Trappani doing the laundry, the boiler hearing the pipes, or the building itself rattling in the cold. But not a train whistle.

Wade propped his feet up on his desk. He could

because he didn't live with his mother. He pulled out the sports page and with a cup of coffee and his biscuit in hand, he turned on the small desk television to watch cartoons. Bugs Bunny. Tweetie Bird. If he was lucky, they would show his favorite with Foghorn Leghorn. Wade's weakness. Wade would try to retell the funny parts of the cartoon to someone, but they would stare at him as if he had a third eye in his forehead, so he stopped trying.

A ball game was coming on at two o'clock and at four he had to go to work. He sat back to enjoy himself in his apartment.

It was a small apartment, a Village apartment. Nine feet across, twenty feet long. The ceiling dropped eight inches from one side to the other. At six-foot-two, Wade could easily touch the ceiling. The shower, commode and sink were all in, his space, so he was thankful for that. A refrigerator, stove. What more could anyone want?

He found all the furniture on the street. His desk, a captain's bed that doubled as a couch. Shelves across one wall were assembled from a friend's excess lumber. The television came from a repair shop that went out of business. Wade waited until the last day before the closing and agreed to take the television. Somebody forgot to pay a $35 repair bill. Wade offered $25 and was out the door. The stereo came from his neighbor, whose friend had died a long and slow death. The neighbor could not bear to set up the system. It was a painful reminder of their friendship. Wade was grateful for the generosity and often remarked how good the sound was or what great reception. The neighbor was pleased and once stated that it was a treat to see it was still giving pleasure. At one time the neighbor did ask to play a particular tape. He talked about his friend for a minute, then took the tape back to his apartment. It must have been too painful.

The desk he found needed sanding and a quick coat of stain. At a remnant store, he bought a rug with thick pile you could grab with your toes. The dinette set with two chairs was near the window and this was his home.

When he first moved in, Wade hung framed photos and paintings on the wall. But after a couple of years, he took them down to paint the walls and never put them up again. He kept them behind the bookshelves and liked the clean look on the walls, painted oyster white. A large wall calendar hung near his desk and two large windows overlooked the back garden. It was a nice view but he had to put up bars to keep out "creepy crawlers."

The front page of the newspaper shows man's failure and the sports page shows his triumphs. In the editorials man talks to himself, and in the comics he laughs at himself. His future is in the horoscopes. Wade's mother used to read all the horoscopes and pick out the one she liked for the day. But she never picked Cancer. "Cancer's enough to make anybody a crab," she would say. She would read Wade's dad's horoscope while they had coffee. It was a ritual and his dad would comment "Really" and that would start their day. Wade read his horoscope and did not believe in its power but thought it was like a lucky charm — best know that it's there.

> Full moon rising. Watch your step.
> Unexpected visitor has news.
> You'll need a uniform. - Libra.

"Oh, really." Wade turned to the sports page. In college, Wade studied business and was fascinated with the stock market and wished that he could "play with the big boys" and trade industries back and forth. The idea fascinated him. He took some of his Granny's money and traded stocks, but it didn't work out. He framed the worthless stock certificates as reminders and kept them behind the shelves with the paintings. Wade believed there was a better commodity. A commodity that reaped better, longer lasting dividends, people. The investment was time. What better compliment to someone than to invest your time with them.

Nothing in the paper caught his interest, so he made his bed and fluffed the pillows. He turned on the television and lay back. The game was starting, but he set his alarm clock for three-thirty. Work at four. History that taught him that odd sleeping hours and a comfortable bed were wrong combinations to keep appointments.

The alarm was not needed, and at three-fifteen Wade made a quick call but nobody was home. He moved to the shower and started his routine.

The Saturday shift began like one of many. Party goers, college kids, uptowners, a few downtowners. The college kids all dressed like slobs. But by dressing in such an unconventional manner, they all dressed alike. The school they attended was the most expensive in the nation. Their parents eroded fortunes so that their children could attend. Wade wondered how the parents would feel if they knew their offspring dressed like hobos. The uptowners all dressed alike, the men, the women, the unknowns. Italian was the design. The men portrayed prissiness. The women looked like linebackers with shoulder pads, shiny black with bangles and close-cropped hair also in shiny black. The downtowners wore dirty black and no accessories.

Black that scientists talk about when they discuss black holes in space. And the downtowners conveyed it in their eyes. The eyes of the college kids had the look of excitement. The eyes of the uptowners darted around the room to see who was admiring them.

The only eyes that Wade was looking for was the blue pair that came in at 11 p.m. She approached the bar from his right side. He did not see her at first because of the crowd. But when he did, he gave her a wink of recognition. She winked back. That was their way in public places.

Her baseball cap with a blue T was set low and only the quick could have caught the wink. She stood patiently as he handed her a glass of wine.

"Will there be anything else?" Wade asked deadpan.

"Not now, maybe later. I'll have something hot." Wade did not flinch. That was the rules of the game.

"Fine. We should have something warm later. It's been simmering all day, and it should be ready by closing time." Wade spoke like a bored waiter.

"Good. I've been looking for something satisfying." She sipped her drink and eased away into the crowd. But Wade lost it. Not publicly, but, inside, his hormones received a wakeup call. All hands on deck, the Navy expression. In the cavalry it is called revelry. Up and at 'em. His body juices were getting a primal call to action. It was Saturday night.

The crowd began to thin when she reappeared at the bar. There was only a drop of wine left in her goblet. Without asking, he poured her another drink. Their hands touched briefly.

"Hello. Do you come here often?"

"Yes, I come ... here often. Could you introduce me to a Libra ... with a big ..." She leaned over the bar and whispered the last word in his ear. She planted a kiss on his cheek and sat down on a barstool. She was gaining points in the game.

"Madam, may I suggest that you try one of the hired help. The liquor purveyor. They say he is a grand fellow and his nickname is ... Sir Lance-a-lot." Wade looked into her blue eyes.

She spewed her wine from her mouth all over the bar. A customer had to jump to avoid the spray. Wade wiped the bar clean and offered the startled customer a new drink. He suggested the lady be more careful. The game had been won.

Wade moved down the bar to tend other customers. Her eyes followed. He loved her eyes, and he often remarked that she could model for makeup commercials or ads for eye glasses. She had high cheekbones and a long neck that he massaged, sometimes with his lips. Her shoulders were soft, and her hair, when let down, would just brush them.

Her honey blonde hair only showed wisps around her ears and forehead. She had it all pushed up under the ball cap. She had just gotten off work. She waited tables at a health food restaurant, and management informed her that her hair would either have to be cut short or worn up. So she borrowed Wade's blue baseball cap and wore her hair up. She could wear anything blue with blue jeans but she hated blue. "Blue is so ... Iowa." But the blue made her eyes shine. She called her hair bottle blonde, but Wade knew differently. He knew.

Her name was Erica. She went by Rikki, and when in a playful mood Wade called her Rikki-tikki. Sometimes, when he held her close and massaged her shoulders he would in his deepest voice call her ... Rik.

This personal interlude from the rest of the bar was an

attempt to hide their relationship in public. But the secret of lovers is open to the public.

"Wade, telephone!" shouted Drew as he held the receiver to his ample belly. Drew, the other bartender for the Saturday night shift took over making the drinks for the uptowners at the bar. A chardonnay and a diet coke.

Wade recognized the voice at the other end of the line as Angela the bookkeeper. She asked that Wade and Drew stick around for a few minutes after closing. She would be right in. Wade passed the phone to Queenie.

"What does that fat butt want? Telling us to stick around." Queenie turned and informed the others that they had to stay after closing. All of them whined and someone stated, "I'm not waiting."

Wade told Drew.

"By the time we get these drunks out of here and clean up, it'll be three anyway." That was what Wade liked about Drew and why Drew got the better Friday and Saturday night shifts. Drew patted his droopy mustache, shrugged his shoulders and wandered down the bar.

At 1:45 a.m., the bar had thinned out and the jukebox was turned off. Wade handed out cups of coffee to the customers. Some refused the coffee, but Wade still put it in front of them. Rikki was seated over at Table 8 with the waitresses and talked shop while Jenny counted the bankroll and Mary Ann folded napkins. Queenie held her clipboard and leaned over the bar.

"It's one forty-five. Angela better show."

"She'll show." Wade assured her, as he wiped down the bar.

Angela had eaten too many muffins. She had eaten too many french fries, burgers, and milkshakes. She drank diet colas, ate diet pizzas and lo-cal cake. Her purse was a storehouse of chips, gum, and chocolate bars. She could recite which foods had the most calories, protein, and at what hours they should be eaten for easier digestion. She knew which foods should be eaten at what time of year. She had summer diets, winter calorie savers, and fall slimmers, plus spring fruit extravaganzas that would help her lose weight. But the simple matter was that she ate and ate. Angela made matters worse by wearing shiny belts, crystal beaded earrings and necklaces that caught the light. Drew thought that was great.

"She could be seen from outer space."

Barry Baseball thought she would be bigger than the Astrodome by Christmas.

She had a problem, compounded by sitting all day doing the books. Angela was an excellent bookkeeper and she moonlighted for other firms around the Village. She had come to the Village to attend school and to work on her novel. But the years passed and the novel never appeared.

Wade nicknamed her Sweetie, because of the chocolate hoard in her purse.

She had a voice of velvet. Sometimes Wade would ask her to call him at home the office if he had to get up early. Her sweet voice belied her huge appearance.

"Good morning, Wade. This is your morning wake-up call. Right now you are the biggest thing in my life." She always mentioned invitations for dinner and suggested dropping by for drinks in a seductive manner, but Wade would always beg off.

"Rikki is number one in my heart."

She was a good bookkeeper, and that was why the bar ran so well without a manager.

Until Angela walked through the door at two o'clock, Wade had no idea who the owner was. He was a disheveled man of about forty-five, who wore a dirty cable knit sweater and faded jeans. His hair looked like a floor mop turned upside down. Angela introduced him as the owner, and he announced that the Rusty Anchor was closed forever.

CHAPTER TWO

Enough

The picture book showed a man with a funny nose and wild gray receding hair. The caption said, “Einstein, the inventor of relativity.” The boy thought relatives came when you were born. Odd that someone would invent such a thing, as his Aunt Clarice and her sloppy kisses. How could you invent a sister whose only words were “Stay outta my room”? His cousin, Peggy, who taught him to dance the mash potato was good and his favorite uncle.

“Understand this, you’re my brother’s boy. I’m part of you, your blood is my blood. I give to you this job.” He grabbed the boy by the shoulders and dug his thumbs into his collarbones.

“Work hard or I’ll kick your ass.” The boy looked down at his uncle’s boots. “Make yourself proud.”

"Yes, sir," said the twelve-year old. Uncle Sam ran the bar in town, Sam's. It was always busy. Twenty-four hours a day. It had no plants, no pretty waitresses or pictures on the walls. It had customers. Always. Sam's was located next to the police station. Every cop, desk commander, secretary, crook, politician, and victim would come into Sam's. He was proud to serve them the coldest beer in town.

"Teeth freezing. I want to see little junks of ice floating on top."

And he served the best stew. That was what he served. The menu had been printed by the previous owner and hung on a blackboard, but Sam never changed it. He just didn't serve the eggs, steak, or fish.

"Hangover Stew" was all he served. Regulars would come through the door and call out, "Hot and cold." One cold beer and one hot stew. No crackers. No bread.

Tourists would complain about not getting what was on the menu and Sam would, "On me," and the customer would stop complaining knowing that he got a free beer and pot of stew. The hot stew would hit the spot and the beer was cold. Sam knew he had a friend, when Sam asked the tourist what he thought about the stew. The recipe was a family secret.

The boy's job was dishwasher, and twenty-seven dollars a week was a fortune. Sam would bring the boy out into the dining room, sopping wet, and introduce him to the customers.

"This is my brother's boy." The boy would dry his hands and squish in his tennis shoes and shake hands with the mayor.

"Works hard."

Frugal was the word for Uncle Sam. Each week on payday, Sam would march the boy to the bank and give him his pay and make him put twenty dollars into the boy's savings account. "College, or you work in the dish room." The twenty dollars was a tremendous amount taken out of the pay, but the frightening thought of the dishroom for eternity made him proud of the savings book he kept under his pillow.

"You got seven dollars left. What you gonna get for your mother?" the uncle asked every week. Dumbfounded that he had to spend money on someone other than himself and with his uncle's thumb digging into his collarbone, as they waited in line and all of the town waiting for an answer, the boy blurted out, "Flowers!"

"Good. Get her candy next week. She's good to you."

Thus was set the pattern: candy, flowers, and a savings account.

One night the boy was asked to stay late.

"You're getting a promotion."

It was the policemen's "Library Night." The police "arrested" Sam for staying open on Sundays. To make bail he had to produce a keg of beer, and the police "booked" the boy for being "related."

The ride out to the fireman's hall in the squad car with the siren on surpassed any thrill. His instructions were direct.

"You're gonna see nothing. Serve the beer. You keep your mouth shut and you get twenty." Twenty dollars! That bike in the window of Newman's would be his. The boy could hardly contain himself. And he saw nothing that he talked about. That week, payday, the uncle handed him his twenty-seven dollars, watched as he placed twenty into savings, then handed the boy another twenty.

"You work hard. Extra. Save this too," indicating the twenty goes to savings. "You get it easier in college. You buying your mother candy this week?" The bike dream disappeared and he answered, "Candy."

On his next birthday the boy was arrested for "walking" to school by the Chief of Police. A stern lecture followed. All "school walking" was to be stopped and the boy should ride this bike from now on ... a gift from the "boys" next door.

Strange are the ways of the world.

Uncle Sam saved his money and bought a farm up north.

"I had enough!" was all he said when he quit the restaurant business. The boy saw his uncle the following Christmas and he seemed very happy.

Time spent with relatives goes slowly. Wade jotted the line into this notebook and poured another cup of coffee. Rikki was seated across the table from him in a bold blue terrycloth robe. He was wearing his green one that she had bought for him. Her apartment was much bigger than his and much more lavish. Thus he spent his time, their time, at her apartment. The couch had blue pillows and lacy curtains. Plants thrived on every table and window sill. Photographs of places she had traveled hung framed on the wall. Her pottery wedged into the shelves among the books. The rug was a wool Persian. The bedroom was a separate room, as was the kitchen. Her apartment was a home compared to his closet. The stereo was playing the local jazz station, but he thought the music was half a beat faster than elevator music. He wanted to play a country western station. Maybe they would play his favorite song by the Jailhouse Whiskey Boys.

"Shot At And Missed ... Shit At And Hit."

But that song revealed how he felt at this moment. "Rhapsody with Xylophone" missed the mood. Rikki thought country western music was "pig yodeling."

Rikki was doing the Sunday crossword and her nails at the same time. Her orange danish and trendy coffee occupied her hunger. It was 1:30 in the afternoon. It had been a long night.

The announcement from the owner of the bar was followed by sounds of astonishment and anger. Drew grabbed his coat and left shouting "adios" as he went out the door. Queenie went into an "off with their heads" routine, demanding to know why, how come.

"Because I said so ... and we're closed now." That was all he said.

Angela was rooting around in her purse for a

handkerchief, but found only candy, so she gorged down a Mars bar. She tried to cry, but food was in her mouth. The owner turned to Wade and asked for the bankroll and the keys. Jenny asked if she could work tomorrow night's shift because she had a doctor bill to pay this week. Mary Ann was crying.

Queenie wanted to sue him, screaming. "We have a right to our jobs!"

When asked what was going to go in here, the owner shrugged his shoulders.

Sensing that to argue was to no avail, Wade reached into the cooler and grabbed a bottle of wine and pulled five dollars from his tips, put the money on the bar. He waved at Rikki who had her cap back on the crown of her head. Her mouth was open. He grabbed his coat and bag and pulled Rikki out the door.

The Saturday night lovemaking was more a war than love. Wade drank most of the wine back at her apartment. Rikki asked a lot of questions, but Wade knew as much as she.

"The owner came in. Closed the bar. End of story."

The answer was not in the bottle but the more he drank the better he felt. After a while she got the message that he was intent on getting drunk. She switched the stereo over to the rock and roll station that played oldie-goldies. Rolling Stone or Beach Boys, if she was lucky. That was the music to get him in a better mood. She knew that much about him. It would have to be a matter of death before she would put on the "pig-yodeling."

"He's putting in a video store!" she offered. Try No. 1. No, there was one down the block. "The Japanese want to open a sushi bar!" Try No. 2. No, too big. You can't open a sushi bar unless the space is equal in size to your closet.

"Then he's putting up condos." Try No. 3. No, who would want to live next to a meat wholesaler?

"Did you get any hints from Angela that this was coming?" She tried to probe, but the wine was racing faster than her questions. He wrinkled up his nose, trying to think.

"No, I placed an order for liquor to be delivered on Monday," Wade answered.

"He could call and cancel," she deadpanned.

"Whose side are you on?" He was past the label on the wine. One sock on and the other under the coffee table. His shirt was unbottoned to his chest.

"I liked the people. I liked that job." He sank lower into his glass and she responded, by massaging his chest.

"I like you, 'cause you like me." That was her phrase to change the mood.

She dug her nails into his chest and her lips into his neck. He found her lips and let her know what was to happen. But it took a while. The wine had its effect that all men are aware of and women must be patient. They grappled on the couch and his pants became tighter and when he tried to take her there on the rug with her clothes thrown around the room and his jeans down around his ankles. The thing that proved he was a man of action decided to be a spectator. His frustration only compounded his inadequacies. He finished the bottle of wine from his prone position and dribbled some on her belly, then licked it up. It was only then that she realized what needed to be done to "erect the situation." Rikki slid out from under him. Pulling him up from the floor, she pushed him into the bedroom and pulled off his clothes, those that remained. She brushed out her hair and unbuttoned her top. She splashed on his favorite perfume and put it places he would be led to. She caressed his thighs and kissed his belly after spilling the wine on him. The wine was pushing him into that state of the grapes, but his senses received the primal wake-up call. His frustration now manifested itself into a mass and after she gave revelry on his bugle, he grabbed her buns and positioned her so that he could deliver his charge.

Wine tickles the tongue but puts the organs to sleep so as he now tried to prove his point that he was indeed alive and not dead, his anger swelled in both heads. His lovemaking became a push and she shoved, he pushed harder and she pulled him stronger. This rocking motion became more rolling and he grabbed her harder on the ass. He pounded and she flopped back at him, until she screamed a sound that he knew she liked, a raw scream of pleasure. He didn't think of baseball to prolong the moment, he didn't bury his head in the pillow and think of some actress with big hair and big teeth. He positioned himself above her and thought of life that now was in full stroke, and he wanted to prove it. He thought of the closing of the bar and the unfairness of that act. He thought of telling Jay that there was no job on Monday. He thought of how he would get another job and that the Rusty Anchor could go to hell. He thought of these things as he kept pushing her and she dug her nails into his back. She pushed harder. He would show her. He would show the world, who was in charge. She screamed again and her body tightened around him. She squeezed and he pushed harder and then his juices flowed in unison with hers. He cussed and buried his head in the pillow and drove three more times. This was "grudge fucking" at it's finest.

When he awoke, she was astride him "riding the stallion." Her long hair was draped over his eyes. Her nails now dug into his chest and left pits that matched the scars on his back. He wanted to scream but it hurt too good. Her movement created pressure on his bladder and thus a "piss hard-on."

"I don't care what's in it, just give it to me." This morning she took.

His wine hangover and cotton-mouth plus that fact that his left arm had fallen asleep made him uncomfortable. This must be what it's like to make love when you're old. Too many pains to feel the pleasure.

He thought of the first time he made love to her two years ago. How romantic it had been. They had returned to his apartment from a late night walk through the snowstorm. His radiator thankfully was working and he offered a cozy cup of hot chocolate spiked with creme de menthe.

"Candy's dandy, but liquor is quicker. You, on the other hand, combine them. I like that in a man."

He winked and it worked. But during the night of lovemaking and three cups of hot chocolate, she got up and opened both windows. In the morning, the apartment and the bed were covered in a thin blanket of snow. Wade was freezing but she thought it was romantic, to make love in a snow drift. Thus she earned her nickname, Snowflake.

"I feel so ... in power, when I'm in the saddle," she said. "Is that how men feel?"

"Yes," he answered.

"I want to ride the stallion more often. I like the view." She cooed.

"Okay, on your birthday." He meant it in jest, but like all men he underestimated this thing called the woman's movement and the sexual revolution. He wanted to sign up as a freedom fighter. A revolution has to have patriots, and Wade was all for the underdog. But she saw no humor in his remark. Right now she really was enjoying the view, and it wasn't her birthday. She was taking the pony down the stretch and like a bareback rider grabbed onto the mane. But this mane was Wade's chest hairs. She crossed the finish line before Wade and held on as his horse came down the back stretch, sore from the night before, but with a thoroughbred's kick. When he crossed the finish line he tried to buck her off, but she held on tighter.

"I need you, Rikki ... you're all I have."

She lay on top of him, not moving, breathing as one, sleeping until noon.

"You were a woolly bear last night," she said as she dabbed a stroke of Lusty Night on her nails. Trading the nail polish brush for a ballpoint, she filled in a six-letter word.

"Woolly bear?"

"You know, all rough and soft at the same time." She got up and sat in his lap. Her robe opening to mid-thigh.

"You made me feel all ... fuzzy inside." She stroked his stubble and asked if she could shave him.

"You feel just fine to me. But I don't know about letting someone fuzzy shave me." He sipped his coffee and she drank some from his cup, even though her cup was there.

"You think this woolly bear could have some eggs? I'm drained."

"Yes." She reached down into his robe to check and squeezed.

"I'll make you three eggs." She went to makc breakfast. He looked at the crosswords. She did the puzzle in pen and drops of nail polish filled some of the squares. He stopped at 16 down.

"Company problem." Six letters. He wrote in "layoff".

"Jay, it's Wade." Wade heard power tools in the background.

"Wade. What's the radar say, my guy?" Jay shouted over the phone.

"Jay, turn the lathe off. I got to tell you something."

Jay did as he was told and came back to the phone.

"Jay, the bar is closed." Wade didn't beat around the bush. Jay asked had there been a fire or a holdup. Wade explained all the details. Jay didn't speak. Wade wanted him to say something, but what could he say. There had been other bars and other crazy situations. This was just the crazy situation of this bar.

"Hey, I'll come over to see your plane, okay?" Wade wanted to end the conversation with happy talk, but ...

"It's not a plane. It's a pterodactyl." Jay hung up.

Wade felt lousy. He looked out the window at the park. He saw an older Chinese woman dressed in parka doing tai-chi exercises. The weather was crisp but she was alone, moving like a single strand of kelp waving in the sea. Wade began to mimic her, slowly stretching his arms and flowing as she flowed.

"Mommy, look at this," he yelled.

"It's a crab. Leave it alone," she shouted down the beach. But he didn't and put it in his pail. The crab tried to scrabble out, but it was too small. Sister was down the beach with the girl next door.

"Looky, here what I got!" He scooped the crab up with his shovel and lobbed it at them. The crab landed on the neighbor's bathing suit and clung for dear life. The boy smiled, but the girl didn't. She screamed and gyrated. The lifeguard, his mother, his dad, and everybody else on the beach heard the screams.

"Dad, it's only a crab," he tried to explain.

"Go sit in the car." Father pointed.

" But, Dad ...."

The boy sat in the car.

The old woman finished her exercises and Wade sat down on the couch. He grabbed a white pillow beside him and felt the embroidered design of a snowflake. He could smell eggs cooking in the kitchen. That was good.

The three-egg omelet was held together with onions, ham, and pieces of apple. It had a taste of cinnamon and the taste of seasalt. Five-grain bread covered with honey, warm from the oven, flanked the omelet. A plate of bacon strips to the right, a shallow bowl of radishes and celery to the left. A cup of steaming mint coffee topped with whipped cream completed the table.

They toasted their coffee cups and winked. Their thing.

"Good morning, wooly bear." She didn't even wait for him as she plunged her fork into the food. Wade had worked in restaurants long enough, eating on the run or snatching bites of food between customers. Now he liked to savor the moment, making a small ceremony of preparing to eat. A little pepper, butter on the bread, a bite of celery to clear the palate. Another sip of coffee to savor, brewed after grinding the beans, superfine sugar sprinkled on the real whipped cream, the subtlety of the mint. Then the move that crosses male-female, democrat-republican, rich-poor, well-bred or boor. A move taught in the first day as a bartender.

Wade swept his arm across the table, grabbed the bottle by the neck, slipped the top with his thumb so it landed in his other hand and poured with the flick of his wrist. A thick red river that plopped onto the eggs and all the male genes in Wade's body knew that the feeding was to begin. Saliva wetted his mouth, his stomach growled in anticipation and his lips smacked. With another quick move the bottle was topped and placed back on the table, exactly in the position it began. Habits formed as a bartender. His food was ready and he dug his fork into the ketchup-soaked eggs.

She saw this through her hair and watched his quick move of the destruction of her masterpiece. Rikki rebelled at such a sight. Just as her mother and her grandmother had, her eyebrows arched, eyes rolled, and followed her mother's pattern and remained silent. But she thought the opinions of every woman since the first meal in a cave when that first tomato was hand-squashed onto a dinosaur steak, "Men are really different."

"That is so trailer court!" The first time she saw him put ketchup on eggs. Her thoughts were of wonderment that this really cool guy, who made her laugh and could make love like she wanted, could be so …

Her mother only replied that Rikki's father was the same way.

"Be thankful he doesn't gargle his milk." Rikki was aghast to learn that her father was so male.

Wade often asked for milk with his eggs but ... "we're out" or "all used up." She crossed her fingers when she told fibs.

Rikki introduced Wade to her patterned plates that she had thrown on a potter's wheel. Glasses that were Irish crystal without cartoon characters, placemats she had made herself while taking weaving classes, napkins that were held by napkin rings, monogrammed silver that was an heirloom from her Granny Mitchell. She appreciated his choices of wine at dinner. He bought her flowers when it wasn't her birthday and when she sensed no guilt. He made the bed as she made breakfast, and he liked to straighten things or help clean up after their meals. He washed the dishes with vigor and she swore he would talk to himself as he scoured the pans. She would ask, but he would be unaware that he was talking to himself. He would clean the tub after he showered, but he had to be told to wipe the chrome to prevent water spots, her pet peeve. She thanked her Protector in heaven, he ate with a fork and a knife. That would be too much to teach. She wanted a man, not a boy to raise.

Rikki loved his mom when they met and looked for traits in her that could help her deal with the son. Cosmopolitan Magazine said that was a good idea. She listened to her with anticipation and, when she got home, checked off the boxes in that month's "lover's quiz." Wade was not "the suave man of your dreams" or "the original Cro-Magnon" but "the All-American guy". If only he would stop with the ketchup. But any man who could make her feel fuzzy and let her ride the stallion was just fine with her.

"He seems nice." Her mother liked all her past men. That's what mothers say.

"What do you plan to do now?" Rikki asked as he wolfed the eggs into his mouth. She waited until he cleared his throat.

"Right now or later?" He raised his eyebrows.

"Later," she replied.

"You and a nap." The eggs took effect.

"In that order?"

She remembered a summer afternoon with the ceiling fan above the bed pushing cool breezes across their bodies.

Bodies, baked by the day at the beach. A short nap was followed by a moment of love that turned the tide of their relationship. Was this to be a short fling or something that would last longer than ice cream in her freezer? Her weakness. Or the current novel she was reading? She would like to have a guy around longer than her shampoo.

He massaged her back with suntan lotion and fell asleep, and when they both rustled awake he took her, again.

She remembered that well, and he said the words. No line. No pauses.

"You are my life." Whispered in her ear. He lay nestled against her body. He nibbled on her lobe and licked the nape of her neck. Then they spooned together and fell asleep.

"And later, after our nap?"

"Go for a walk. It looks pleasant outside." Wade chewed on a piece of bread lathered with strawberry preserve.

"What about work?" She poured more coffee.

"Something will pop up. Always has." Wade was concentrating on his bacon. Crisp strips dried with a paper towel. "Might take some time off." The thought did appeal.

"You already got it." Coolly.

Their nap was slap and tickle playtime. Wade showered and remained in his robe as they cooked up some pasta and set up trays to watch a rented video, *Bulldog Drummond.* They retired about ten as was their pattern.

Monday. One eye opened and he scratched an itch on his chin. Wade wondered where he was and then realized he was on Rikki's side of the bed. He went to sleep on his side, after taking a slice out of the middle of the bed and her. But the sheet was wrapped around his legs and as he climbed out of bed to adjust the blinds, he landed on his hands and knees beside his robe and her slippers.

"Good morning," he said to himself and looked across the bed to see if he had disturbed her. Rikki did not move and he unwrapped his blanket and the fixed the wayward slat from the blind that allowed the sunlight to illuminate the bed. In two minutes the sun would be kissing her cheeks and her hair would be truly gold. She looked so angelic. He wanted to crawl back into bed, but his body clock said, "move it."

The shower was the best part of her apartment, besides her bed. It was an old four-legged cast-iron tub with a spray nozzle that would peel paint. The hot water was always plentiful and the bathroom itself was always warm due to a steam pipe running beside the towel rack, not only making the room toasty but the towels as well. He put the shower on full blast and scrubbed his body with the Imperial Leather brand soap that he kept there. Rikki like the little decorative soaps that she kept in wicker baskets on the shelves, but Wade felt that they were perfume not soap. If he didn't use some sort of industrial strength soap to fight the odors of his body, he would end up smelling like a goat.

But right now the hot water pulsated onto his spine and he wriggled his back so that the water column hit the sore spots. A little flab was gathering at the love handles, but he felt that he could wear that away with some summer sports, such as basketball or baseball. He was proud that his gut still was flat and that his pelvic bones protruded further than his stomach. He lathered up and turned towards the stream of water to rinse his body and froze. That sound again.

"Rikki?" he called out over the sound of the water. He drew back the shower curtain with the huge snowflakes on a blue background. She was not there and the sound had stopped.

This tub had seen some fine moments, he thought. Countless residents through the years, love, death, even candle-lit baths with her. But trains do not run through this bathroom, nor do haunting train whistles exist in showers. It had to be the pipes; water running through the pipes creating a sound like train whistles across the prairies. It must have something to do with water pressure, divided by the resistance of the material of the pipe, and the inverse relationship of the pipe's diameter. That must be it. He didn't take physics in college for nothing.

There it was again, that sound. He cleared the soap from his ears and listened. The water spray spilled onto his chest. It was a train whistle dropping in tone and then reaching a frantic height as if there was a car on the tracks and the engineer was letting the world know what was coming. Wade listened to catch the full effect of the sound. It dropped in tone and faded. He stopped the shower and stepped out of the tub to dry off.

The streets were empty except for a couple of cabs cruising like sharks looking for a meal. An elderly gentleman, wearing an English bowler hat and carrying a cane, tipped his hat to Wade.

"Good day".

" Yeah right." Wade whispered under his breath.

As he climbed the stairs to the landing, he saw that the door to his apartment was open by about four inches. He noticed right away that a burglar had been there. The window on the fire escape was up and a pane of glass in the upper sash had been smashed to open the lock. His camera was gone. His clothing was all there but the stereo, the television, and the change on the table were gone. Wade opened the refrigerator and lifted the ice tray in the freezer. Five one-hundred-dollar bills. Cold crisp cash.

To call the cops would be a lesson in stupidity.

"Lucky you weren't home," the officer would say.

"Why?"

"He might have killed you."

"If I was here the burglar would not have robbed me. I wouldn't stand around and point out my valuables. I would have clobbered him."

"Then we would have to arrest you for murder."

"Someone steals my things and I get arrested for preventing a robbery?"

"Yup. They got rights."

"What have I got?"

"Problems. If he lived, he could sue you."

"Which is better?"

"Shoot to kill. Save us the paper work. One less piece of scum."

"Thanks." Wade had heard the line before.

Wade sat down at his desk and looked at the window. His bowl of change was gone. It was a bowl she had made for him, and he placed his change. His goal was to wrap the coins, and take her to Disneyland. The bowl was about ten inches across and eight inches deep. Almost full. Rikki asked about the change bowl Sunday, as she emptied her change into a five-gallon glass water jug. Rikki had taped a picture of Tinkerbelle on the bottle. The collection came up to the slippers.

"This summer," she said.

Disneyland would have to wait. Wade sipped on his orange juice and opened his notebook.

"Mom. Mom, look at this. I found it out back."

The boy clutched the thing in his hand. She turned from the sink with its never-ending pile of dishes.

She wiped her hair from her forehead and looked down at the grubby little hand that held something.

"Open your hand and let me see."

He slowly opened his fingers, and a baby snake fell to the floor and slithered toward his mother.

"Get that thing out of here. Get it out of here." She jumped up and down like a pogo stick.

"Mom, it's only a baby snake." He reached down and retrieved the reptile and walked out the kitchen door.

He petted the snake and tenderly placed it back where he had found it in the tall grass. With a crayon he crossed out his sign that he had written on a cardboard box.

World's Greatest Snake — $5

Wade decided that deciding was the wrong thing to do at this moment. He gave up thinking. It was too hard to think. His brain hurt.

In the second grade, Wade wanted to be a cowboy when he grew up. But his dad wouldn't buy him a pony. He could keep it in his room, he protested. No pony.

By the fourth grade, Wade wanted to be a nuclear physicist. No one else could spell such words or knew why physicists wanted atom bombs when everyone else was building bomb shelters.

But it sure sounded good. Besides, John Hartman wanted to be one.

In junior high school, Eddie Kinney, who came to school in a wheelchair, taught Wade how to play chess. Eddie had a chemistry set in has bedroom that served as the dayroom for the family. Eddie showed Wade some chemical reactions, but mostly they made hot chocolate on the Bunsen burner. Wade could be a chemist and play chess all day. That's what Eddie wanted to do and that sounded pretty neat. Back then, neat was the word. One day Eddie didn't come to school. When Wade went over to his house, Eddie's mom said he had died. She gave Wade the chemistry set. She was happy that Wade had come over and had been Eddie's friend. But Wade never opened the chemistry set. It was Eddie's.

In high school, Wade thought he would be a doctor. Wade had broken enough bones in sports, and Doctor Culpepper was a great guy. He owned his own convertible, which was great. Great was the word then. It predated groovy.

In his senior year of high school, Wade discovered the stock market and invested his "Granny money" with a stockbroker, who was cool. He made money both ways, buying and selling. Wade decided he wanted to be a stockbroker.

But the stock went straight down and he lost his grandmother's money.

Bummer.

In college, the counselor asked he what he wanted to do. Wade didn't know.

"What you do like about life?"

"Girls. Money. Travel. Fame."

The counselor lowered his eyebrows.

"What am I supposed to know? I'm seventeen. I spent the last twelve years stuck in a classroom."

"How about English 101?"

"Far out, man. Four more years sitting in a classroom will help me 'decide' what I want to do in life?"

This was the Age of Aquarius.

The counselor suggested some psychological testing. But the multiple-choice indicated that Wade should be a carpenter. Colleges don't graduate carpenters. Four years later with a degree in hand, Wade knew two things. He wanted out of college and he was broke.

Free at last, free at last.

For four years there had been "Peace, brother" and "Right on," but that was all forgotten. The word was … job.

Ten years after graduation, the word was still … job.

"Daddy, can I help you building something?"

The boy pulled a little hammer from his Handy Andy tool box Christmas present.

"Not now, son, I got to build some shelves for mother."

The dark basement was a storehouse of treasures that could be nailed together, old plywood scraps, two-by-fours, one-bys. The boy moved to the corner and looked at a wooden box that held an old folded blanket. This was Kelly's box. But Kelly, who had been raised from a puppy, was confined to the yard while the men of the house worked. With hammer and bent nails and some pieces of wood, the boy set to work. After supper he scooted back downstairs to finish.

As Dad finished sanding the shelves and began putting his tools away, he asked his little carpenter about the oddly constructed project that Kelly was growling at.

"It's a dog. For Kelly to play with."

Kelly immediately did what dogs do to fire hydrants.

Wade finished writing in his notebook and pondered his life, his travels, his accomplishments, his total being.

"I built a dog."

CHAPTER THREE

The mail brought with it the mailman. Who brought with him his attitude and the earplugs to his radio. The mailman shuffled the letters like a card dealer, hummed his tune and vanished. Once Wade left a package in the mail box to take upstairs. The mailman quickly chided Wade for occupying government space and Wade vowed never to do it again. Since then, he has readdressed all junk mail to the postmaster general.

He could pay the rent, the gas and electric, the phone, but no long distance. What else could he do? The cold cash was gone and money lent to a friend returned. He didn't want to borrow money from his credit card but his options dwindled fast. His credit limit was now a fantasy and he hadn't paid his bills in two months. They were sure to put him on the most wanted list. Finally, they sent him a letter with one sentence.

"If you use the card again, you die."

Rikki offered to lend him some money and hinted that two could live as cheap as one. That wasn't they way he wanted to make the jump — with a pocket full of lint and a mouthful of "gimme." Her reply was that she earned good money and her apartment was inexpensive and roomier than his cubbyhole. He thought of the day when he would ask a lady to be his mate and companion but he wanted to do it on his own terms, not under duress, financial or otherwise. Rikki thought they could live on love.

"Mommy come see my fort."

Mommy entered the cardboard box leaning against the tree. "Mommy, this is my fort. But no girls are allowed."

Three other boys all cramped inside the fort smiled back from their crunched up position.

"I'm a girl," Mommy said.

"No you're a Mommy."

They passed the cookies around and traded baseball cards. Mommy sipped the Kool-Aide and looked at the comic books.

"You like the Lone Ranger, Mommy?"

She nodded and told the story of great-grandpa meeting Wild Bill Hickok.

"Boy, you sure are great, Mommy."

He hugged her and asked her to come back tomorrow.

"Maybe."

But she never did come back to the fort. And the next weekend the rain soaked the cardboard box and it leaned over and looked like a sick mass of goo. The painted sign on the side now ran together and "Fort XXX—NO GIRLS." Now read, "FoX LS."

He told his aunt about his fort and she said build a bigger fort in the trees. But summer came and went and he never did.

The gray of the winter sky was seeping into Wade's apartment. His budget said pennies and his cupboard said oatmeal. It was easy to cook but Wade got tired of looking at the old geezer in the funny hat on the box. Rikki offered to cook and he accepted a couple of times a week but it was hard to reciprocate with drinks out.

His desk became a pile of business cards and old phone numbers that he had collected over the years. He called every restaurant person he knew and checked the want ads. He asked about business and confirmed what they heard about the Rusty Anchor. He thanked them for their good wishes but, no work.

A lot of that going around.

It was the fever all right. No hundred dollar doctor's office visit, to confirm the obvious. Wade's head was a pool of mud that dribbled down his noise. His shoulders ached like a tired old highway. His throat felt like gravel. But the pain was the cost of the pills. Fifteen dollars for the blue ones. Three-fifty each for the red ones. They didn't work.

The medicine that worked, vodka and orange juice.

"A little sunshine and a little pain killer." His grandmother's remedy. She was 85. She must know something.

Wade lay in bed and tried to watch tv, but the little black and white set just couldn't get the picture together for some reason. The talk show host looked better with squiggly lines across his face than the three pounds of makeup to hide his crow's feet. His guests were, "Mother who wanted their daughters to have guns", and he constantly bounded up the stairs of the audience, brushed back his hair and picked obvious "plants" who would incite the group and up the ratings. The soap operas were worse. The problems of those people were fantastic, and eventually Wade found himself involved, waiting until the next segment, worried about James, Ellen and Bill and on and on. But the stories were nauseating—so much so that he turned the tv off.

Besides he had his own soap opera.

"Will Wade find work in the decade?"

"Will he recover his strength?"

"Will Rikki love him knowing he has a cold?"

Wade stopped talking to himself and stopped fantasizing. He realized the pills and the soap opera were mixing with the vodka.

His pillow was hard as rock. He tried to sleep but his stomach churned and his eyes felt like lead. The sheet wrapped around him like a python death grip. The mattress had no soft spot and the blanket felt like a piece of plywood. Thus was his third day in bed. Rich man. Poor man. Health is everything.

"Mommy, I don't want to go to school."

He was shaking. His towel was wrapped around his shoulders, and he didn't care if he was exposed.

"You feel hot."

Mommy touched his forehead.

"I'm sick."

"Okay, get back to bed, and I'll bring you some porridge. We'll put some Vaporub on your chest."

"Mommy, hot chocolate would make me feel better."

She nodded.

"I want my mommy."

Wade sat up and shifted his legs to the edge of the bed. His arms felt like they couldn't lift a feather. He stood up and put his hands on the bookshelf to steady himself. He slipped into his loafers. And put on another sweater. Then his jacket, his gloves and his ball cap, pulled low. Wade traveled down the steps to the front door. As he passed Mrs. Favarucci's apartment the combination of the smell of last night's pasta and the rolling motion, his first in three days, he threw up in the courtyard. He was surprised that anything was able to come up. He tried to make it to the garbage can, but the lid stuck and he blasted the top of it and himself. He jumped back but some landed on his loafers. Two, three times he urped. Dry heaves. That feeling of pulling the stomach up. Finally he came to his senses and brushed himself off and went over to the hose and turned on the nozzle. He sipped, cleansed and spit. Again. That unforgettable taste lingered. Again. Then he took a long sip from the stream. Why can't you get that taste from your own tap? Rubber hose water. The taste reminded him of summer.

Wade noticed the mess on top of the garbage bucket and turned the hose over to wash the lid off. The water splattered over the lid.

Morgan, the graduate student, who lived next door, entered the courtyard and saw the stream of water splashing on the garbage cans.

"Bored, are we?" And left.

Wade went outside. The fresh air felt good. He walked easily. He was weak. His hat was pulled low so that no one would know who he was. He headed to the Panic.

The Panic was a pastry shop on West Fourth Street with glass block and black decor. All the help shaved their scalps on the left side and put earrings in their lobes. Each round earring would turn on its axis, and the boys, if you couldn't tell (the blue earrings) had "pain" written on them. The girls (pink earrings) had 'pleasure" written on them. Sometimes Wade felt that the wrong people had the wrong earrings. But what they did have was hot chocolate steamed with milk, cinnamon on top, in a container for a dollar.

"Thank you, Mommy." He sipped on the cup of love and sat on the bench outside the door. A steady stream of customers came and went. Wade did not notice who sat beside him.

But the feeling of dread came over him. His shoulders shook and his neck tightened. His jaw clenched. A drool of snot leaked out. He wiped it away.

"Wade?" She spoke softly.

"Are you all right?" It was the voice of a nurse, but the face belonged to Queenie.

"Wade, I was worried about you since the Anchor closed." She turned to the newly seated friend.

"Jimmy, look it's Wade."

Queenie sat back and Jimmy leaned forward to see Wade. Wade cocked his eye.

"Wade, guy, how you doing?" Jimmy extended a hand, and Wade noticed that there was no grease on his hands. His nails were clean and the cuffs of his shirt actually looked as if it had been cleaned. His outer coat looked like a jacket, as opposed to a gas station coverall.

"Sick. Got the bug." Wade eeked out.

"Wade," spoke Jimmy. "I'd like to thank you for

introducing me to Queenie. She has changed my life in these two months. I guess we should be going? Right, Sugar Buns? We are handing out Bibles for the Church."

They both stood up and Queenie waved off with hellos to Rikki. Wade sat on the bench for a moment then upchucked some more. A waiter came out with a bucket of water to splash down the sidewalk. He looked at Wade and asked, "Anything else?"

Wade walked up West Fourth, one block, past a mustachioed man, wearing a tweed snapbrim cap, glasses perched on the end of his nose and an army jacket, leaning against the wrought iron fence. The man said, "Books," as Wade passed, implying books were for sale in his apartment but with the secrecy of a marijuana sale. Wade responded, "Television," turned and walked down toward the river.

The Rusty Anchor was a spooky sight. Bottles were on the bar. The floor was not mopped. The chairs were not up on the tables. The table where the girls had rolled silverware was as if they just left. A pile of mail was pushed through the slot and laid on the floor. A graffiti artist had painted "Jett" on the side of the building, but the Anchor retained its name, just a little more rust.

"Mommy, who is that old man?"

Mommy edged closer to the bed and held the hand of the boy. With the other hand, she touched the hand of the sleeping man.

"Dad."

The old man opened his eyes and saw the young mother.

"Dad, this is Wade."

Mommy pulled the boy toward the old man who lifted his hand from the bed. The nails were white as the skin and the veins gave blue streaks toward the fingers.

"This is your grandpa."

The old man touched the head of the boy and patted.

"I got no hair. Feel."

The boy touched the hair but it was thin and slight.

The old man asked if the boy wanted gum and proceeded to bring out a stick.

"Tear it in half."

The boy did and Mommy left the room.

The boy sat on the bed, chewing with his grandpa.

Neither speaking.

"Bye, Grandpa." Wade pressed his nose to the window one last time. The clock was running inside. Some far distant waterfall tumbled down a canyon into a beer can colored in neon.

The breeze from the river was tainted with a mixture of salt and garbage. A tug pushed a three-masted sailboat. Some joggers ran along the water's edge. The traffic on the street picked up as those scurrying to and fro were now going fro.

This street or highway, as the Village residents called it, was the busiest section of the Village. But half a block up at the curb was an old blue Chevy pick-up truck, half on the sidewalk, half on the street. A pair of legs stuck out from the midsection. Wade kept walking.

"Wade. Wade." The voice crawled out from the truck and up stood. Henry extended his hand to shake, pulled it back and then wiped with an oil rag and offered again.

"I saw you walking from under the truck. You must be carrying a lot of cargo."

Who would know more about walking, than a Navy man who has to balance his life as he crosses the deck?

Wade muttered that he was sick. Henry offered a garlic and orange juice concoction that might do the trick. Family recipe.

What family? Wade thought.

The wind picked up as Henry talked about his truck. And how it had carried him from Miami when he got out of the Navy and was the last vestige of that trip. He was determined to keep it going. Henry invited Wade to sit in the driver's seat and feel the wooden wheel. The seat was restored leather and the headliner was baby blue. Not a splotch or wrinkle.

This was the first time he had sat in the driver's seat of a car since the summer. You walk in the Village. The dials on the truck looked archaic. Gas. Speed. Battery.

Beauty in its simplicity.

Wade climbed out of the truck.

"Interested in working, Wade?" Henry blurted.

"Yes. I'll take any job that you have."

"Well, before you take the job let me tell you about what we have."

"I need to work," Wade said forcefully.

"Wait a minute. The job means that you have to come in to work at four in the morning, work 'til noon."

"I'll take it."

The deal was done. Oil or no oil on their hands, Wade and Henry shook.

The first thing … Wade had to tell Rikki. Your best friend, your best girl, the person who was part of you. Who else do you share with? Sometimes when he slept in his own bed, he could feel her, but she would not be there. They had become one. She eats, he eats. He sleeps, she sleeps. He laughs, she laughs. She cries, they cry. But now the good news was here. To hell with four a.m.

I have a job.

"Dad, look. Dad, look."

The boy raced home from school, report card in hand.

"I got a B. Look, I got a B."

The father put his paper down and looked at the report card. He patted the boy on the shoulder.

Mommy came from the back bedroom.

"Be quiet. Shhh. Your sister's crying in the back."

"Why, Mommy?"

"She got a B."

The creaky stairs up the two flights were taken in a quick step. The ratty old building didn't smell that bad. The dingy apartment looked okay. Clothes that were piled beside the bed on top of the magazines and books were brushed aside.

The phone was here someplace. And the time was right: 7:15 p.m.

Over the years that they had dated, Rikki and Wade had decided to call each other only at 11:15 a.m., 3:15 and 7:15 p.m., so as not to bother each other. If they did not connect, each would think of the other at those times, communicate telephonic or telepathic. Rikki believed it worked. Wade believed in Rikki.

Coyly, he asked if she had had a good day. Would she care for a glass of wine? A short one. Wade hung up the phone and grabbed the last of the orange juice from the fridge. A quick hit from the bottle. His cold was gone. He breathed in. Again. His arms still felt weak, but he could breathe.

Rikki's building was not far and as he approached the vestibule, something darted from the garbage cans to the left. Wade jumped. It was dark. Furry. Probably a rat. Wade tried the front door and then heard the "mew." He looked to the garbage cans and saw an orange and white face jut out at him.

"Hello." Bending down, Wade extended his hand and the kitten came from the garbage can. "You're friendly." Wade patted the kitten and it balled up in his palms and licked the salt off of his hand.

"No!" She said no two or three times. Wade pulled out a saucer and poured some milk.

The kitten was an orange and white with big feet, a black spot on his right shoulder, a tiger stripe and a black foot, a true calico. He walked right into the saucer with his front feet and began to lap. Wade pulled out some ham strips from the refrigerator and placed them beside the saucer. "We'll try and find the owner and if not ..."

They moved to the couch as she opened the wine and eyed the cat with milk all over its face.

Her day had been okay. This was the day for her gynecological exam. She dreaded it and put it off. Wade tried to understand, but men never realize the vulnerability that women feel.

"You put your feet up in the stirrups. Feel the breeze. Hoping that this isn't the day that Sal the carpenter, decides to barge in and fix the shelves while you're up like this." Rikki raised her legs but of course she had her jeans on. She brushed back her hair. A shower would make her feel better. The wine was helping. Wade began to tell his story and when he got to the point of the job offer, Rikki and Wade jumped up and down in the living room. They hugged and kissed for the ordeal had ended, until he told her about the hours and her face went funny.

He explained and he figured that they could spend the afternoons together. No change, just early to bed.

Wade opted to sleep at his house that night, due to remains of his cold and Rikki offered the extra alarm clock. That's what he liked about her; she was practical.

"Put this clock across the room. Use two alarms. At that hour you could turn off the first alarm and go back to sleep. This is the shotgun that will wake you."

And she was right.

When he returned home, Wade cleaned his apartment and folded his clothes, pulled out his cleanest slacks and a white shirt. The black and white checked tie. He placed them on the table and shined his shoes. He cleaned the dishes and brushed his teeth. He wore his tartan robe around the apartment. It wasn't as luxurious as the green and black striped robe that he left at Rikki's. That was the most beautiful robe in the world to him because she told the story of trying it on in the department store when she bought it during the past Christmas. He thought that would be a funny sight.

Wade set the alarm, but sleep evaded him. He had been sleeping for the last three days, on and off. Now, when he needed to sleep, he couldn't. His thoughts were of that first bill he could pay, a bottle of wine for Rikki, maybe a night out at Paul Revere's on Barrow. Paul Revere's was the finest of the dining establishments in the Village. The piano player sat in the window. The cherry wood panelling, fireplace, floral displays on the bar. Waiters in tuxedos. Cut crystal glasses and bone china plates. A corner booth. Candles. Champagne. Rikki deserved to be wined and dined.

"I'll bet the food is so good … it'll make you cry."

The clock said eleven. Wade got up and watched the news. No news is better. The sports report was the same tripe. A prima donna of the grass wanted respect and more money. The weather report, partly sunny, which is an optimist's view.

Eleven thirty. The Honeymooners. He had to watch this show. Wade had watched this show for years and this time he concentrated on Norton. But when Cramden said, "Baby, you're the greatest!" Wade smiled and thought he should say that to Rikki tomorrow.

Lights out.

Wade dreamed of driving a car, but it only had three

wheels, and as he drove the car he had to lift the back end of the car. He drove the car down a long winding road that led into a black tunnel and his car was going faster. Driving and carrying the car, Wade headed into the tunnel, but as he did a long loud roar chased him out. Wade woke to the sound of the alarm.

Three o'clock. Wade reached out and turned off the alarm. He hit the light switch on the reading light and lay back, but the "shotgun" went off on the table, so he had to get out of bed to turn it off.

Standing in the center of the room, Wade looked at the clock. He had a job, and this was day one.

"What have I done?" he mumbled.

"Not hungry," he said.

"Your mother cooked a good meal. Eat, son."

"Not hungry. Dad."

"Son, something troubling you?"

"No."

"No means yes when you say it that way. Did you wreck the car?"

"How did you know?"

Daddy thought for a moment.

"This is the first time you've done it."

Showered, shaved, dressed. Wade grabbed his bag and left the apartment. He felt as if he was going on a date. But at three in the morning people are coming in, not going out. The street was empty. The security patrol made up of geriatric vigilantes crept up the block. In packs of five, they wandered the streets of the neighborhood, each waving a flashlight, seeking bad guys.

The canopy of Sixty-Six was dark green and covered the sidewalk. The building rose straight up to the stars. The glass doors were massive panes that held goldfish as door handles.

The lobby was aquamarine with twin pillars in the center. A doorman's booth was to the side of the inner set of doors. Henry could be seen through the doors, sitting at the booth. He buzzed Wade in.

Henry poured a cup of coffee from the urn beside the booth and wrote in the logbook that Wade had check in. He poured a cup for Wade and the caffeine took effect immediately.

"Do you want to drop your bag? We got lockers for ya in the basement." Henry locked the front door and put the sign out for the tenants to buzz if they came in late. Henry's office was eigth feet by eight feet. The back wall behind his desk was a pegboard of keys. The right wall was clipboards and the wall to the left of this desk was shelving stuffed with the remains of the world. His desk had two broken locks and door handles and a pipe wrench held down some papers. His chair was brown leather cracked up the spine. The chair looked very comfortable, despite the aging; it rocked back and forth of its own will. Henry plopped down in the chair and twirled. He picked a key from the pegboard for Wade's locker.

"You'll look good for a doorman. We got new uniforms coming today. The owner didn't like the navy blue coats and gray slacks. Something new."

Wade found his locker in the basement beside the carpenter shop. He grabbed his bag and went back upstairs.

Henry was letting in a young woman who was kissing her date goodnight. Henry logged it in the book and began instructing Wade how to be a doorman from four until noon.

The mail went here, newspapers there, the packages here and the drop-offs here. Henry explained the odd bits of the job and a few rules that might apply. But the effect of a cold and lack of solid sleep over the last few days made the coffee pot a nice center of attention.

5:30 a.m. "Nineteen fifty-six, I was on this tender that served the South Atlantic fleet. Did my time in the service and mustered out at Miami. You go into the Navy, Wade?"

Wade shook his head no.

"Good food but rough life. Always away. Every time you come home, your wife presents you with a new kid. Got to a point where I wanted to come home, you know, but I ... we couldn't afford any more kids." Henry and Wade laughed a locker room laugh.

“How many kids you got, Henry?” Wade asked as they stood beside the booth. Three residents had come in and been logged.

“Five. My oldest boy went in the Navy. You know what I missed most when I was at sea?”

Wade shrugged.

“Home. The face of my wife. I learned the value of being with her. We been married a long time. She’s as mean as a snake.

“Has to be … to keep me in line. Now, I sail this building.”

“Well, I’m one of your sailors, skipper.” Wade saluted.

“You got a girl, Wade?”

“Yes, I do.” Wade was proud that he did have Rikki.

“Good. Makes for better workers. Rule Number 2. Don’t go upstairs to party.”

6:00 a.m. The elevator began to “ding” as it came to the lobby. Wade looked behind him and bodies began to scurry out and head for the door. Wade propped the front doors open and a cool blast of fresh air came into the lobby. Wade recognized a few people and said hello. Good morning. Beautiful day. The pace quickened in the lobby and Wade felt good because now he was working. Before he was sitting.

Work defines us. It makes us breathe and Wade filled his lungs.

Hello. How are you? Good morning!

7:00 a.m. The dog walkers came and went. Poodles pranced from the elevator and peed not ten feet from the door. Shepherds slopped their tongues dangling at one end and a tail at the other. A boxer named “Max” pulled its owner, in silver slippers, a gold robe and sunglasses out the door. “Who are you?” sniffed a retriever that circled Wade as the owner took his time from the elevator.

“Fred. Fred McIntosh. You must be the new doorman.

“Good to see a new face around. Welcome aboard. This is Hank. He’s a good dog. Friendly just likes to sniff.” Fred and Hank went to do their business.

Henry shrugged his shoulders and stated that the building had a lot of friendly people. Some of the dog walkers returned with papers under their arm and some returned with coffee and a bag of pastry. This was the morning ritual.

A few employees arrived and Henry introduced them to Wade. He tried to catch their names, but he knew that would take time.

“Wade, I’m going down to the office. You can handle this for now. Buzz me on the phone if you need me. Look over there.” Henry pointed to the corner of the pillar top.

“That’s a camera. If you need me in a hurry, just wave.” Henry got up and Wade sat down on the stool.

She sauntered in. Her shoes were two-tone and her socks were mismatched. Her dress was a patchwork of colors and her coat was covered by a shawl. Her hair had streaks of blue and gold and her nails were each a different color, chewed to the quick. Her lipstick was black and her eye shadow was blue and red. Her eyes were green. Her complexion pale, her shoulders slight. Wade stood and asked her name, and she said, “Sheliah.”

“May I help you?” Wade stood over her.

“I work here and this day shall be known as the day we crossed the line.” Sheliah exhaled the cold air from the outside and walked to the basement door at the rear of the lobby. The phone range and Wade picked up.

“Lobby.” Wade listened and turned to the camera on the pillar. It was Henry saying he should have told Wade about Sheliah. She works in housekeeping. Wade hung up the phone and pulled out his notebook.

“Top of the Irish to you.”

Daddy spoke in brogue. As he jiggled the covers to wake the boy.

“What’s the Irish, Daddy?”

“Why, son, they are the leprechauns who play tricks on people and help you find the pot of gold.”

Daddy said, as he helped him tie his shoes. “And today is their day.”

“I want a pot of gold, Daddy,” the boy said.

"First, you find a leprechaun and they will lead you to the end of the rainbow. There you will find the pot of gold."

"Daddy, how will I know I've found a leprechaun?"

"You will just know, son."

Wade stretched his legs by walking around outside and helped an elderly tenant get out of a cab. She was apprehensive, but Wade introduced himself, and all was okay. The mail came and boxes were dropped off by the delivery service. Flowers for someone in 13G. Laundry and dry cleaning for 12F.

11:15 a.m. "Rikki." Wade used the lobby phone when Henry came up for a moment. Rikki sounded cheery and asked Wade about his job. They decided to meet for coffee in an hour, and Wade would buzz her up at the house.

"What did you name the kitten?" Wade asked.

"Frisco." Rikki chose that name because the kitten had played all night on the bed keeping her awake.

"Call him Frisco Fred." They good-byed.

"Junior works the noon-to-eight shift. He said he would be late so you can take off at noon, Wade. I'll fill ..." Henry looked over Wade's shoulder to the street. A black limousine pulled up and Henry knew who was inside. He grabbed the paper towels under the desk and gave the coffee machine and doorman's booth a quick rub and trashed the last cup.

"Go help him in. He might have some stuff." Henry pushed Wade through the doors and disappeared to the back of the lobby. Wade approached the curb and opened the door of the limousine. A large bag of clothing was pushed out and voice followed.

"Grab this. What took you so long? Ten seconds from the time the car stopped until the door opened. We provide service, not excuses." Wade grabbed the bag and offered a hand to the person connected to the voice. But it was not accepted.

"I'm not a woman, you idiot."

But how would Wade know if the windows were tinted. You drive around in darkened cars because you think you are important, live in secluded mansions because you can afford them, and when no one knows who you are, you are mad.

But Mr. Alvin Murkoff was important. He owned the building. He owned the sidewalk Wade stood on. He owned this limo that Wade had just opened. He signed the checks to an army of employees, and Wade was now standing face to face with his new boss.

Murkoff's clothes were Italian, made this week by a designer who would be popular next year. His shoes were English, made by a company with two names. Each name cost a hundred dollars. His tie was silk, but his face was granite. A shock of hair ringed his face because his dark complexion gave him the look of a perpetual three-day beard. The hair on his head jetted with gray at the temples, but was black as coal and parted down the middle. His eyebrows did not play along the contour of his face and arch up but stuck straight out from the socket, as if he had plugged himself into the wall unit.

"Who are you?" Murkoff asked as he unfolded from the car. "Where is Carl?" Murkoff looked Wade into the eyes and waited.

"'I'm Wade, the doorman. I'll take your bag inside." Wade turned and walked inside to the rack beside the doorman's booth and hung up the clothing bag. Murkoff followed Wade indoors and looked at Wade standing at the booth.

"Get Henry."

Wade turned and waved at the camera. He looked at Murkoff. If Murkoff was to throw a punch, Wade thought, it would be his last because a roundhouse to Murkoff's nose would crush his breathing capacity. Wade clenched his fist.

Henry came up from the basement and entered the lobby through the back door. He walked towards Murkoff with his hand extended. "Mr. Murkoff. Did you meet Wade?"

Murkoff nodded and turned toward Wade.

"The new uniforms are in the bag. Go put this one on. I want to see what it looks like."

Wade turned and grabbed the bag and went down stairs to the locker room. As he descended the stairs, Wade thought that he could avoid this clown since he worked the morning shift. Maybe this job might be okay. Plus, it was almost noon and time to leave.

The carpentry shop door was open and Doc was working on a lathe. Wade didn't remember his name when he was introduced earlier, but as he walked into the shop and the whirring of the lathe obscured his footsteps he saw his overalls hanging on the door and his tag. He was bent over the wood that turned and he held a chisel with both hands and a cigarette dangled from his mouth. His glasses collected the bits from the wood. Wade watched as he moved the tool over the wood, and sawdust gathered in his gray hair like gold flakes into the snow. Finally he stopped and looked up.

"Banister for 11E."

Wade nodded.

"You work with wood?" Doc brushed the sawdust from his hair and lifted his glasses.

"Some but not serious. I can pound a nail," Wade said.

"We take carpenters very seriously around here," Doc stated. "The three most important people in the world were carpenters."

"Who?" asked Wade.

"Me, 'cause it pays my rent." Doc flicked his fingers as he counted.

"Richard Burbage." Doc paused for Wade to recognize the name. Wade did not.

"Burbage built Shakespeare's stage, the Globe. Dreams

come alive on the stage."

Wade nodded.

"Our Lord Jesus Christ was a carpenter." He flicked a third finger.

Wade nodded.

"There is something about working with wood and mankind. I'd like to know what it is. What is the secret that makes them both work. Do you know, Wade?"

Wade hemmed and hawed, erred and then blurted.

"Patience?"

Doc nodded.

"You can come into my shop any time. Help yourself to any tool you want. I'll give you a key next time I see you." With that Doc turned the lathe back on and lowered his glasses. He looked at Wade and lowered the chisel into the wood. He then winked and over the roar of the lathe shouted.

"Women. You need patience with women."

There are times in one's life when action is just followed. Thoughts are put aside. Opinion dispensed with. Discretion thrown aside. Wade tried to remain composed. Composure is collected inside the skin and held.

As he ascended the stairs from the basement and passed through the lobby, he stopped at the wall mirror between the elevators and looked at himself. Murkoff and Henry looked at him and came closer. Neither said anything. They did not get too close.

It was a good thing. Wade was tired. He stood erect but he knew he was small inside his frame. His eyes looked into the mirror and only at his own eyes. He did not look down.

But Henry did, and Murkoff did too. They saw the new uniforms of the doormen of Sixty-Six, the new impression that would greet the residents in the morning, at night, and in the eyes of Murkoff, the world.

But Wade saw something different. Fire engine red tunic with gold trim up the side, gold cuffs and gold buttons. Gold epaulets extending halfway down the biceps and gold trim at the collar. The hat had a black visor, the peak was six inches above the visor, gold trim on the brim and a nautical crest at the peak. The design over the heart was that of a fish coming out of water, similar to the door handles.

Standing straight, Wade pondered his fate and thought he could apply to some Latin American country, as a dictator. But knew that this was his new uniform and he was the ringmaster of the circus.

CHAPTER FOUR

The envelope was brown. A manila material with a flimsy little window that showed his name and address. Wade tore it open and looked at the amount for six days of work. The amount, minus taxes, did not flatter him, but the fact that he got a paycheck did. It had been months and when Henry handed him the envelope, he felt good. He was working. Alive. Wade folded the paycheck and put it in his back pocket.

The shift was just starting and "8-to-4" Steven said "hello-good-bye." Steven did not speak much, other than, this package was here and that was there. But it was four in the morning, so he went downstairs and changed and out the door. Wade locked the doors after Steven and looked around the lobby. He felt a shiver and the lobby felt cold, empty. He turned to the coffee pot. Steven had unplugged it when he had vacuumed the lobby. Easily remedied.

The blinking lights of the Christmas tree gave a nice glow. It was a real tree and the aroma made Wade breathe deep.

Tomorrow will be the longest night of the year, Wade thought. Wade was going to take his money and buy Rikki's

Christmas present. His desire was to buy something blue with love but with his paycheck he could only afford toast. But he had Rikki, someone to share the lights with. He looked toward the front door and across the street an old man walked by, dragging a small cart. Wade watched him walk towards the bus stop and sit in the bus shelter. Wade tweaked the coffee pot as the last drop came out and he settled in on the stool and pulled out his notebook.

> "Jingle, jingle, jingle." He snorted and scratched his beard and then his ribcage. The salesman had seen his type before, especially the breath.
>
> "Six weeks ago, turkey, turkey, turkey. You liquor guys invented holidays." With a flourish he reached into his vest pocket and pulled out a dollar crumpled more ways than an accordion. The salesman sacked the bottled eggnog and put the change into the register. He wished he could disinfect the money first. His hands he could wash.
>
> The old man wandered out the door. His name was Creston, by age, 62 … by miles traveled, 80 … by the lines on his face, 100. Creston was limping into the night with his little cart and fingerless gloves. Down the street,

crossing at the light, he went over to the bus shelter. It would be warm. He could see the traffic and enjoy the night air.

Because it's cold doesn't mean it's not pleasant, he mused.

He noticed the pedestrians rambling by. They only wore one coat. Ludicrous. This is winter. Being no fool, he wore long johns, a Tiger's T-shirt, a long-sleeved shirt, and two sweaters, a spring jacket, a pea coat, a trench coat, a wool cap and hood. Cozy and comfy, he sat down.

Reaching into his coat, he found the can opener. From his sack he found the can of Del Monte peas. He took a sip from the eggnog and opened the can. He scooped the peas into his mouth with the opener and savored every pea before he swallowed. He thought of the peas all day, then swiped them from the deli. Peas, green, round. Garden marbles. He finished the eggnog and the alcohol swept over his body. He snuggled into the corner for the night.

The Christmas lights signaled someone else's birthday. There were no lights for Creston, for it was his birthday, too. Praying as he always

> did for forgiveness of his sins, for the peas, for the eggnog, and for those that had less than him at this time of year. Creston prayed for his deliverance through the night.

Wade closed his notebook and pulled out his mystery book to read. He looked at the chore list for the night and sipped his coffee. He took out his sweater and pulled it on. His tunic jacket was hanging at his side in case he should have to put it on if Murkoff came in. He loosened the shoes and flicked some lint away from his pants. The tenants thought the outfits looked stupid and a petition was started to get the navy blazers back. It may happen but until then, the doormen suffered. Wade put down the book and looked at the clock.

5:00 a.m. The book was Agatha Christie's *Murder on the Nile*. How odd, he thought, that an elderly lady of means would write about murder and gore. He couldn't image his Aunt Mary and Aunt Jean sitting around the tea service.

> "Jean dear, pass the marmalade for the scones, please. I'm at the point in the book where Master Tommy has delayed his life long enough with Miss Nancy and has decided that Miss Lea would be a much better partner in love."
>
> "Astonishing, Mary, since Sir Reginald's

money merely sits in trust at Portman's Bank for Miss Nancy. More tea?"

"Master Tommy could easily send Miss Nancy to her reward with his Chamberlain .004 gauge partridge gun that he picked up at Lorraine and Singles, the shop for distinguished sportsmen."

"Is that on Chester Road in Derby?"

"Yes, dear. One lump or two?"

"Miss Marple could catch them in Marabella and send him back to the Tower, held for trial, hanged by the neck until dead."

"A just reward for malcontents, Mary."

"Another cookie?"

Wade put his book down and unlocked the door and went out for a fresh breath of air. Down the street towards the river he could see a neighbor walking up the middle of the street singing a liberated song pushed out by whisky and strained by years on the vocal cords. As he passed Wade and turned into the building, Wade caught his arm and insisted that the singer lived across the street. But the singer persisted that he lived here. Wade could bounce the guy like a ball because he was older and the ravages of liquor had reduced him to a rail, but he was a neighbor. He merely held on to his arm and hoped that the singer didn't throw up on his shoes.

"Say, I can have you fired, you'se know?" His bourbon breath blasted.

"Sir, that may be, but you live across the street. In that building!"

Looking for his keys like a fifteen-year-old fondling his first set of breasts, the singing neighbor leaned over. Wade thought, this is it. Here, on my shoes.

"My keys are in my socks."

The singer began stamping his foot like Trigger counting to four.

"I keep 'em there in case I have a good time and forget where they are." He wiped his mouth on his coat sleeve and the keys jingled to his feet.

"There."

A folded cocktail napkin, very moist, fell to the sidewalk.

"I need that. That's the most important piece of paper in the world. My new sweetie gave me that in the bar. I am in love."

"Good way to be," Wade said and picked up the paper and put it in the pocket of the neighbor.

Ernie, the doorman across the street, saw the commotion and had crossed to the curb.

"Must be Tuesday." Ernie grabbed the singing neighbor by the tie and led him across the street.

"That the new doorman, Ernie? Nice guy. Gotta buy him a drink."

Wade went back to his book. It had flipped a page, but that was okay. Ernie waved through the glass doors, and Wade gave him the thumbs-up sign. Thumbs up. The last time Wade went jogging was thumbs up.

The chore list for the "4-to-noon" shift was short. But the night mail delivery had to be put up. Sacks of mail delivered by a service, dropped off, then put into the mailboxes.

Wade liked the job because he knew it was the quickest way to learn the names of the tenants. Not that he was a snoop, but in the soap opera of life, this was the quickest way to learn about their hobbies, their spending habits, their lives. Apartment 18G was having a birthday. The multicolored cards came from the corners of the globe. Mort Whitcomb.

Mort Whitcomb was a columnist for The Times. Wade had not seen him yet, but his picture was in the paper everyday. Alongside his by-line … "Mort … Warts and All." Wade sorted the cards and thought about his own birthday a couple of months ago, when things were good.

"Mommy, how old is eight?"

The boy held up six fingers.

"When I'm eight, do I get eight cards from Grammy?"

Mommy nodded.

"Do I get forty when I'm forty?"

Mommy giggled. The boy opened the

card.

"Daddy, read it." Daddy read.

"What's the Mutual 'surance Company?"

"It's a card from the insurance company."

The boy smiled and had some chocolate cake and looked at the card with the "5" written on it.

But they didn't remember his birthday when he was nine. When Wade graduated from college and it was mentioned in the town newspaper, the insurance salesman called to talk about an interesting financial package. "Now that you're starting out in life."

"No." Wade hung up the phone.

A card at nine would have been paid back in time.

Everybody has a birthday, unless you're dead. Dogs have seven a year. Cows have two. People only have one.

"I am as old as Jack Benny," Granny would say.

Poor Methuselah. What would you give a guy who had 900 birthdays?

Water-skis? "No, thanks, the pair I got when I was 372 are fine."

A sweater. "Got plenty."

Bow and arrows. "Got one when they were first invented."

Guitar. "No, thanks, Nero gave me his."

Wade promised to make a list of his friends and family and be more diligent about birthdays and shuffled the last of Mort Whitcomb's cards into the box. The list would start with his grandparents, his parents and siblings, and then his uncles and aunts.

Rikki would be easy to remember because he marked it on the calendar, and she had the peculiar notion to celebrate her "half-birthday."

"I made it half way," she cooed with pride.

"Reward yourself." Wade would suggest a bubble bath. Pedicure. Massage.

"Let's go out and have a bottle of wine." But Rikki would suggest staying around the house. The practical side of her would prevail.

Wade thought that the greeting card industry could make a gold mine from selling half- birthday cards.

"I'm seven and a half." Sister said.

"Mommy, tell her she's still seven." Brother said.

"Seven and a half." she sang

repeatedly.

"Mommy, can I be a half now that I just had a birthday?"

"Yes."

"Are you a half, Mommy?" They both asked.

"No."

"How old are you, Mommy?"

"Twenty-nine for the rest of my life."

"Wow! Mommy, that's old!"

With that the broom lifted from the floor and tykes were sent to watch tv.

Wade closed his book and kicked off his shoes and scratched the heel of his foot on the rung of the stool.

"Good pair of shoes will take care of a man's feet."

The voice came from the bench to the right of the booth. It startled Wade and he stood up. Wade immediately recognized the man. It was Mort Whitcomb.

"Man's feet carry him through life."

Mort sat cross-legged and lit his cigar. His glasses gave him a bug-eyed appearance. A red tam sat on his head. His white shirt was open at the collar and half way down his chest. Part of it was tucked in his beltless pants.

"What are you writing?" Mort asked.

Wade closed his book and put it in his bag and said

nothing.

"That's how I started. Wrote a diary about how I hated summer camp and gave it to my mother. Didn't go to summer camp the next year. 'Cept mother never believed there were dragons with green eyes in Lake Wikiwakken."

Mort got up, produced a cup and poured from the coffeepot by the booth. He stood as short as his name.

"These shoes," pointing to his shoes that were brown with white paint splotched on them, "have been around the world. Luckily, I was wearing them. Got them in Albuquerque. Still got desert in them. Look."

"I believe you," Wade offered, but to no avail.

Mort took off his shoe and poured white sand out of the heel into the cigarette canister that held more white sand.

"I was telling you a story about these shoes. Now if you don't want me to tell you ..." Mort sipped from the cup. Wade nodded.

"Albuquerque. Nice place. Got some good friends there. Now Albany, different place altogether." Mort flicked his cigar.

"Needed some shoes in forty-one. Depression and all. Course, I had to go to boot camp to get them. Army paid me two dollars a month. Lost it all in poker. If I'm sixty, I'm sure of one thing, young man, poker is where men are tested." Mort's eyes bugged out waiting for an answer.

"Dice. Not good with cards." Wade played dice in

college, a faster game.

"Dice! Riskier than cards.

"Dance with Lady Luck, get your toes stepped on!" Mort admonished Wade with his cup.

"Army had me writing stories for their magazine, The Bugle. Now a true reporter would write stories to boost morale ... how to fix a jeep, how to shine boots. But I told whoppers, fish stories, and little fibs about the generals. Editor couldn't fire me. I was drafted. Couldn't put me up front, I wore glasses." Mort pulled from his cigar and looked out the window. The night was being chased by the morning.

"I've done a lot of things. I've gotten drunk in Tangiers. Been inside a Mexican jail. Tamed tigers. Ate alligator. And chased girls. I've seen the mountains and lived in the desert. Swam all the oceans, watched the sunset on every continent. One thing I haven't done ..." Mort's voice rose.

"Paid a nickel for a beer. I was born too late and missed the mother lode of the century."

"Sorry, Mr. Whitcomb." Wade offered condolences.

"Mort. Mort. Everybody calls me Mort," he stated.

"My name's Wade." Wade raised his coffee cup.

"Mrs. Donaldson, on the fourth floor, thinks you're a spy writing down our lives in your notebook. Course, Mrs. Donaldson would easily flip over to the other side if they bribed her with cable." Mort sometimes referred to Mrs. Donaldson in his column as Lotta Axtogrind, the mother-in-law. Wade giggled and checked the clock.

The dog walkers came and went. The early risers scurried out like dice from the cup onto the felt, then stopped in the glare of the big casino at the curb. Yesterday had crapped out and it was seven-come-eleven today.

The newspaper delivery came and dropped off about 125 papers. Mort went to the pile and pulled his out as Wade stacked them in numerical order, then reached in and opened one, flipped to the column Mort had written for the day.

The premise was that Mort had invited Atlas, the Pope, Winston Churchill, Babe Ruth, Eve, Geronimo, Marilyn Monroe, and Helen of Troy to dinner with the express purpose of convincing Harpo Marx, the guest of honor, to make the toast. Mort never revealed who would have convinced Harpo to talk, the reader had to provide the answer.

"Who?" Mort asked when Wade read the column.

"Helen of Troy," Wade offered.

"You're a sucker for a pretty face!" Mort giggled.

"Yeah. They cost me a bundle. What I do fall for is someone who is my pal, my lover, my confidant. It takes a long time to find that someone. And when you do, the first lesson is to go slow, until they become part of you. Too much, too fast, fades quickly. Better to be a slow-growing ember than a shooting star in the night."

"Wise words, Wade, but sometimes it doesn't work out that way." Mort lowered the tone of his voice and looked into his coffee and saw the past.

"Wade, have you seen the movie 'Casablanca'? That movie depicts all there is in life. Love. Mystery. Death. War. Double-dealing. The triumph of good over evil." Mort continued talking. "I had the choice of going to the USO or seeing "Casablanca". Figured I had a better chance at the movies than with all the other GIs at a dance. Sat in the back row and kissed her on the lips."

Wade smiled at an era when a kiss on the lips was a pretty serious situation.

"Scum, he called me." Mort stood up. "Her father called me scum because I wanted to be a newspaperman. A man of the pen is not scum!" Mort's indignation was as fresh as it was many years ago.

"Writing lives forever!"

"Mort, that was years ago. Her father was probably worried about the life a writer would provide. You should have written a letter to convince her that your heart was true. It would have shown her your feelings."

"I never did." Mort sat back down and looked out the glass doors of the lobby.

Wade sipped from his cup.

"She was a cute little butterfly." Mort got up and went toward the elevators, then turned back.

"You are right. The answer is Helen of Troy. She could make Harpo Marx speak. Any woman that could launch a thousand ships and have a guy fight ten years for her, could make any clown talk."

Wade laughed and turned towards the booth. He checked the clock and poured some more coffee and opened his notebook.

Across the fields of floral rainbows

Blue above, terra green,

Wiggling gaily, giggling flowers,

Kissed sunbeam soft,

Chuckle chatter of laughter

Climbs cooling winds

And tells the timbers

It's time for the dance of the butterfly.

Impatient imps adding waves to wiggles

Kisses to giggles

A blessing on their two lips.

Life in the Garden can be so sweet.

Each sighs as she kisses and dances on.

Brief. Beauteous. Rewarding.

Rapturous.

Exhilarated, the children sigh,

And beg for more.

In a delight, deaf to their sighs,

Humming to herself,

She dances beyond their dreams.

Kept among the stones

Thrown by giant hand,

Cold perches. Hard rock.

Podiums for singing squirrels,

Boulders bounce light away.

A yellow petal seeks the light

Above the grass of summer.

Taught by the leaves of fall,

Asking why, beneath the winter snow,

Reborn in the winds of spring,

He endures.

With added height

Above the rocks

A reward for his patience,

A rainbow meadow before him,

Tranced. A throng of tempting
tempura

Trounces his mind.

He dreams only of sunlight,

Something he saw above.

This vista humbled him.

"There is beauty."

The butterfly danced to him.

Spellbound by her hum,

He blinked not an eye

As she kissed his petals.

Away she danced to the imps.

He spoke,

Life was dismal.

Now I see beauty, my reward.

Away she dances, for another day.

To keep her would destroy her

And all her light.

I wait. If she returns

She shall be truly mine.

Good-bye, my sweet butterfly,

Return to your Dandy Lyon.

The morning routine began as the mail came at ten and the workers checked in. Henry buzzed up a couple of times from the basement and asked if Wade wanted some extra work next week. Doc lingered around the doorman's booth and talked about how some trim needed to be redone in the lobby. He then asked Wade to stop by the carpentry shop after twelve when he got off. Wade put on his tunic and looked at himself in the mirror.

Murkoff was expected and Henry did not want to take any chances. The final hour crept along very slowly, as time does when tomorrow is your day off. Wade opened his notebook and recorded that he had to do laundry. He wasn't used to wearing a clean white shirt every day and his ironing is not that good, but he was learning.

Junior, the "noon-to-8" doorman, walked quickly through the front door, down the stairs and reappeared, dressed and ready to go at 11:55. He would say he was fifty, but he was lying.

"Lie up on your age, people get impressed on how good you look." He had a commanding presence although he was not as tall as Wade. It was his shoulders. At a younger age he could have been a tackle on the team, but now he had a pot belly and a receding hairline, so he looked more like the coach. But he always came to work eating a box of popcorn, so he had become a "fan." He had a slight Southern twang, and always offered the box of popcorn.

Henry once alluded to the fact that Junior lived next to a movie house and spent all of his nights there.

"Junior, you ever see 'Casablanca'?" Wade asked.

"Boring. No monsters. I can see all that here in this lobby." Junior probably had, since he worked there for eighteen years. Wade pointed to a pile of papers that was to be returned or messengered and then he signed out of the logbook. Grabbing the last of the mail, Wade put it under the doorman's booth and saw a package for Mort Whitcomb.

"Mort." Wade knocked on the door. "It's me, Wade, from downstairs." Wade didn't hear anything and leaned over to put the box against the door, just as Mort opened it. There in his splendor, wrapped in a towel, his cigar and his tam, dripping wet, stood Mort.

"Box came in late for you, Mort," Wade stammered.

"Thanks, Wade." Mort fumbled with his towels and the box.

"Wade, writers never take showers. Do all your good thinking in the tub. The water cleans the pores and the steam clears the coco-noggin." Mort tapped his head. With that, he closed the door.

Wade went downstairs by the freight elevator that opened across from the carpentry shop. Wade entered and unbuttoned his tunic.

"Grab yourself some coffee, Wade," Doc offered. Wade was coffeed out. Doc was over in the corner of the shop where the furnace chimney came up from the floor below. It was bricked and heat still poured forth, making the carpentry shop very warm.

"Gotta do something about this heat. What do you suggest?"

Wade suggested extra asbestos and another layer of brick.

"That's too easy." Doc smiled. "Wade, do you know what the Idle Tire Act was?"

"No."

"That's the problem, and we are going to correct it."

"We?"

"We are going to build a space to remember. Or more exactly, we'll put stuff in a space to be opened years from now, and people will find stuff from today." Doc put his hands on his hips.

"I think they call them time capsules and they open them every hundred years. But down here in the basement, the only person to open it would be a plumber," Wade deducted.

"Exactly. We would be communicating with a carpenter or a plumber of the future."

The space was about ten by four by two feet, and a lot of stuff could be put in there. Doc laid out his plans and explained that the Idle Tire Act was designed by the government during the Depression to pay people to save rubber. Small certificates were handed out with a quarter, which was a lot of money. Doc wanted to put his collection of certificates in the time box, to tell people to conserve.

The plan was to bring up extra bricks from the furnace room in the subcellar and start collecting stuff for the time vault.

"Wade, I want you to catalog all this stuff. Maybe they won't know what this stuff is in the future. We may have to include a diagram or instructions. It will be our secret."

"Our secret." Wade was intrigued.

At the deli, Wade ordered a liverwurst and cheddar with onion on rye, with a root beer to wash it down. He crossed the street and climbed the stairs to his own apartment building. No doorman greeted him, and no carpeting eased his tired feet. No potted palm added a little green in the lobby.

This squatty old building was an old warrior whose battle scars were inflicted by drunks, children, flying skillets. It had been painted more times than a hooker. Its floors sagged to the weight of newlyweds and retirees marching up and down the stairs. Young singles planning sexual skirmishes. An old woman of the night recalling many raw recruits, she ushered from boyhood to manhood in her boot camp sessions. A pony player as big as Man of War. Lonely gays, who weren't so lonely, as their doors cracked open and young men slipped in and out like spies. Battered by life's shells and too proud to fall, the old warrior just squatted, a warrior with no fancy name, but still on duty. The landlady whose English was lost, but not her heritage. She offered homemade wine that would kill a brigade in exchange for light bulbs changed.

"You'se tell me if anything is broken. I got a hammer. Very nice."

His apartment was dimly lit. He hung up his tunic and pants. He stripped to his skivvies and checked the clock to make a call.

"Helloooo." He mimicked her when she answered the phone. She had just got up. Rikki worked the restaurant last night and he could picture her in her robe. They decided to get together later. On his desk, Wade had a clipping of Mort's column.

Mort wrote about suits.

It seemed the rock group, Tatting Crayons, with a lead singer known as Turtle Nose, was performing in town. Mort remarked that the Crayons wore their underwear outside of the clothes but sang songs about virgins. Politicians had zippers that could not stay up. Athletes had so many logos and patches on their uniforms, when, Bomber, the Home Run King, recruited from reform school, on his way to the Big House, swung the bat, it looked like a series of commercials. And those who wore power blue suits, but had none.

"We say … 'all over him like a cheap suit'. Why don't we say, 'all around town like an expensive suit'?"

Bankers wear brown suits. Shifty guys living in hotels wear brown suits.

"Nobody wears vests with gold watch chains," he lamented.

Mort closed his column. He would rather be a doorman, in an outlandish uniform, than a yes man at the top of a glass tower.

7:15 p.m. Wade called over to Rikki's and she was ready to go. He buzzed her apartment and she came down the two flights of stairs to the door. Her hair was down and the cool breeze of winter, swirled her curls. She grabbed the collar of her coat and stuck the muffler around her neck and under her chin. She pecked him on the lips, but Wade grabbed her by the waist and held her, then gave her a good kiss.

"You look like you needed that," he stated.

He put his arms around her shoulders and they wandered down the street under the canopy of empty branches.

If it was a movie, the camera would travel through the open doors of McCasey's, a small pub in the Village. The camera would reveal Wade and Rikki sitting at their favorite table along the wall to the right of the bar. The lights would rise and music lower, the sound of giggles as they replayed their week, without each other. They would toast over beers. And the candlelight would sparkle in her eyes. The warmth and coziness of the pub would make them draw closer as they ordered their burgers and rings.

Rikki referred to them as brick burgers because they sat in her stomach. The extra slab of cheddar cheese had plenty to do with it. Nibbling on her fries, she told of Frisco Fred, controlling the house and sleeping on her chest in the morning. The stupid hours of bed at eight-thirty and work at four had cut into their time. Wade should ask for different hours soon.

"Things are getting better. It's just good to be working again. The hours are killing me too. Be patient. Please."

Rikki reached over and touched him on his hand.

Wade talked of meeting Mort and hoped that Rikki could meet him soon. Maybe have dinner with him. Wade talked of Doc and his plan to build a time box for the future. But Rikki didn't understand the purpose of putting it in the basement.

"As good a place as any," Wade said. "Doc wants to communicate with the carpenters and plumbers because they haven't changed in time. These men, in a pub, that their grandfathers built, they may be hoisting beer, but they are trying to carry their world on their shoulders."

"Atlas?"

"Yes. Praying that the weight of jobs, family, mortgages, with a light paycheck, doesn't break their backs. These men have not changed since the time of the ancients."

"But do you think that a hundred years from now, a bunch of carpenters will be interested in the artifacts that are put into a time box? Beyond baseball, beer, and women, how much pleasure would they get from anything else?" said Rikki.

"Okay. We'll put in a six-pack, baseball schedule, and a girlie magazine." He paused. "And the complete works of Shakespeare."

"What?" She gave a quizzical look.

"Well, there are women carpenters and plumbers. What would you put in?"

She thought for a moment and said she would think about it.

They finished their burgers and had another round of beer on the house, sent over by Drew, the bartender from the Rusty Anchor.

Wade saw him when they came in but he was too busy to talk. Drew stood six feet four and his face mirrored the five years in the Marines and an additional twenty behind the bar. His drooping mustache matched his eyelids and the droop over his belt.

"Buffalo Bills will kick ass." He said as he pulled up a chair and said hello to Rikki. They toasted their glasses. To Drew there were two fields of valor, the gridiron and a faraway battlefield where his leg was shattered leaving him with a limp. He didn't talk about the field of valor on an oriental peninsula, but if he sized up a customer who had not served on either field of valor, their conversation would be cut off.

"You've never tasted combat." He would shout out

and the customer would slink out the door. But if you served on a gridiron and knew that fourth and three was a gut wrenching play up the middle then you were served.

Drew knew victory on a foreign shore was assured by the lessons learned on cinder fields, frozen by the harsh Lake Erie wind. Boys with no padding, slim futures and minimal guidance were later taught to kill. Victory was not sweet when a teammate lay twisted in agony and death. Drew, Wade and Rikki toasted in remembrance creating more “dead soldiers”.

“What would you say to a carpenter, a hundred years from now, Drew?” asked Rikki.

“That I was glad to be here!” Drew sipped on his beer.

“No, what would you tell him?”

“That the Buffalo Bills had won a bunch of Super Bowls. Beer prices had gone up. The girls were still pretty. What would you tell him?”

“Or her.” Rikki interjected as she looked at Wade.

Drew leaned back in his chair and twirled his mustache and continued.

“I would hope … we could figure out this thing called love. Hell, they might call it something else by then!”

“Don’t think so,” added Wade.

“Well, whatever. Life and love go together and we spend too much time alone.”

“Drew, you’re a romantic,” Rikki said.

“No, I am a bartender.”

"Wade is the poor man's cupid! He likes to introduce nice people to other nice people."

Rikki smiled as Wade began to blush.

"Hell. He should go on tv. Write a book about it."

"He does write," Rikki said. "So what would you say to someone, in the future, with a broken heart?"

"Have a cold beer. If she really loves you, she'll come to her senses. And if she doesn't, have another beer. We'll find someone nice for you. Put a quarter in the jukebox."

"Sounds like good advice. Does that apply to women, too?" asked Rikki.

"You bet. Most of these guys in here are ordinary guys. There is no book to go by. They aren't Prince Charming. You wait tables, you see plenty of guys and they hit on you. Why do you like Wade?"

"'Cause I feel comfortable around him. I can be myself. It's an easy pleasure to be with him."

"What if you lost him?"

"I'd pray held come back to me." Rikki looked Wade in the eyes.

"Baby, you're the greatest!" Wade reached out his hand, grabbed hers and kissed it.

"My work is done. A hundred years from how there will be a nice couple sitting here, and I hope I will be a bartender to see this beautiful sight."

Rikki and Wade didn't see him leave as they sat looking

only at each other in the candlelight.

Later, as they walked home holding hands and giggling, they passed a table of jewelry set up on the sidewalk by an artisan. Rikki handled a couple of pieces and put them back. A puppy sat in the artisan's lap, and Rikki reached out to pet the puppy.

"That's a beautiful piece." She pointed. A glass triangle was handed to Rikki from the back row on the table. It was on a leather thong strung with blue beads.

"It's a snowflake that I saw in Washington state. I carved it out of glass and sunk it in more glass," the artisan said.

Rikki put it over her head and the snowflake rested between her breasts.

"It's a booby knocker."

Wade laughed and paid the man his price.

"Merry Christmas, Rikki."

She wrapped up her coat with the jewelry next to her heart.

Rikki used the bathroom first while Wade took off his coat. Rikki emerged from the bathroom with his robe and handed it to him and tugged at his belt. She was already in her robe. She turned on the stereo and lowered the lights.

"Let's dance."

Rikki held out her arms and Wade stepped forward. Her body was firm and he could feel the booby knocker under her robe. Rikki snuggled closer and rested her head on his shoulder. Wade put his arms completely around her and then she undid his robe to seek out the heat of his body.

As Bobby Darin sang the last chorus of "Beyond the Sea," they stood motionless and that was how they danced the night away.

CHAPTER FIVE

They slept like the proverbial bugs in a rug, for the night air had cooled the apartment after they had heated it up considerably. Rikki pulled down the comforter and they huddled under the blankets. At 3:30 in the morning, Wade woke with a start and looked at the clock. He put his arm under Rikki and she hummed a little and snuggled. Both went back to sleep.

Here's to sweet repose.

Belly to belly,

Toes to toes.

Here's to sweet delight.

Fanny to fanny,

The rest of the night.

"Can I be your friend?" she cooed.

Wade opened his eyes and looked at her. The sun was just coming into the room. It was 8:30 a.m.

"Yes. But you were my friend before you were my

lover."

Day 1.

"Hello," he said.

No answer as she stood in the bookstore.

"Um, do you like books?" he asked.

No answer.

"Well, maybe I'll just talk to myself. I like books. They are my friends. They talk to me … listen ..."

She listened as he squeaked the story of Goldilocks and the Three Bears.

"Now, do you like books? You can answer when you stop laughing." He walked away.

"Yes, I like books," she said, as she approached.

"Do you like coffee?" he asked.

No answer.

"I can do a great imitation of a coffee bean, but you'd be embarrassed in front of all these people."

There was no one in the store.

"Okay. Coffee down the street."

"Good. My name's Wade."

"Rikki."

And they walked out into the rain.

"When are you going to visit your parents for Christmas?" Wade asked.

"Next week. I'm taking a bus. I want to see the country. You never see anything in a plane."

They chatted over breakfast at Maurico's. The back garden was open because the temperature was slightly spring like. But it was empty, a prime requirement for them.

"Did you get your shopping done for your grandparents?" Rikki asked as she slurped her coffee and some whipped cream lingered on her upper lip until her tongue found it.

"I don't know what to get them. If they wanted something, they go get it. If they need something, they already have it. What do you give old people other than a smile? What do they want other than to see their kids do well? They can't eat cheese or cookies. They don't drink, other than a glass of sherry on the porch. They have sweaters and they barely use the things we give them year and after year. They have all the photos of us. Tea cozies and knickknacks. They have everything." Wade sipped his coffee.

"Except their youth."

"They have their memories. Better than gold."

St. Valentine's Day

The old man leaned on his cane as his companion of many years helped him to the head of the table. He whispered in her ear.

"I love you so much I could spit."

"Watch your tongue." Grandmother pointed to the boy.

She placed a napkin under grandpa's chin and the boy did the same. Flowers were in the center of the table and candles at the sides.

The old man began by eating his squash. The ham and brown gravy would wait.

"Grammy, can I have some more yammies?" the boy asked. Grandpa smiled.

"Jeebees, child, don't you eat."

He did eat, but the plate of cookies by the flowers had his eyes.

For dessert, the candles were lowered and plates were removed. Grandmother brought out scoops of vanilla ice cream from the kitchen. The plate of cookies was moved closer to the boy.

By nine o'clock, Grammy and Grandpa were both asleep at the table, and the boy continued to eat the cookies.

Two Valentine cards sat in front of

Grammy, one from each of her true loves.

"What sort of memories would you like to have of us?" Rikki dug her fork into eggs.

"We never seem to argue. So, I don't remember any tiffs or spats between us so far. Nice memories."

"So far. No discussions." She toasted her cup to his.

"They're fights to men, but discussions to women." Wade put down his fork.

"I'd like us to hold the line, for now. This job is okay, but not good. Things can get better. I don't have a blueprint of life, but I'm sure you would like one." He giggled.

"No."

"Oh, come on. I can't even take you out to a restaurant, as a surprise, without you asking where, why, what, when!"

"I like to be ready."

"Well, I guess someday, when you're ready, the natural course of life would be ...."

"The natural course of life?"

"Well ... I guess ... I might see something …"

"Something. What?"

"Well, if I saw something like a small house, somewhere. A cottage, because we definitely aren't suburbia. And you liked it ..."

"And I liked it?"

"Well, the means to get it might appear. Just like anything

else in life. I guess if it had some bedrooms and they were empty, I might put my arms around your shoulders and say ..."

"And say?"

"Say ... 'Rikki, do you think we could ... a couple of children to fill these empty rooms'?"

"That's the natural course of life, you think?"

"Yes. What do you think?"

"Where is this cottage?" she asked.

"I don't know. But it'll be ours for a long time."

"I'd like to live by the sea. With a cat named Sage and a dog named Pepper. Maybe a goat named Zephyr."

"Okay by me."

"Maybe a few trees, with the sea beyond."

"Fine. It's out there somewhere. We'll know what we want when we see it."

"When?"

Wade giggled and Rikki picked up the giggles as she realized she was doing exactly as Wade had predicted.

They parted after brunch because Wade had things to do on his day off and Rikki decided to go browsing in book shops in the Village. It was her thing and Wade was always amazed at how much she enjoyed it. At first, he thought she was going with the girls for lunch and gabbing. But she said she always went alone. It was always a pleasure to talk with her on the days after she book shopped. She seemed so exhilarated. Even though they had met in a book store and he did enjoy going occasionally, it was her thing. Best not intrude unless asked. Besides he got the benefits. A new Rikki. Fresh. Excited. Talkative.

When Wade got home he read Mort's column for the day and clipped it.

> Even now after many years, I remember Kenwood Junction. To forget would eliminate pleasant memories of days filled with love, people and moments that can never be replaced. At times I think of the trees in this small village.
>
> The majesty. Elms. Maples. Pines. Spruce.
>
> Trees as solid as the word of God.
>
> Evenly spaced on both sides of the street, these trees reached toward the heavens, protecting the children below, holding the grass in place. They gave shade to swings and laughter.
>
> The grass, rich and luxuriant, was everywhere. Grass, that tickled your toes and carpeted the world of Kenwood Junction.
>
> Soft. Summer green. Running from the street to the garden's edge. Marigolds bowed to its expanse. Grass that became part of the children as mothers washed green knees and feet

at day's end.

Sidewalks were solid paths from neighbor to neighbor.

Homes with cookies in the cupboard and kitchen tables with fresh-cut daisies stuffed into a water jug. Refrigerators hidden by kindergarten doodlings and moms with blue-checked aprons handing you a glass of lemonade.

Angels would sigh and play their harps, bringing cool breezes and fluffy clouds to the sky. I remember this village and with the help of God, someday may I go there.

Wade wondered about the column. No one was butchered, skewered or barbecued. To be mentioned in Mort's column was something, even if he served your head on a platter, a national one at that. Last month, the reigning cinematic siren, Mort referred to as Boobie Fillet, who had the morals of an ashtray and the IQ of a salt shaker, went on national television and gushed about the review Mort had given her latest movie, but she missed the point. Wade would ask Mort about the column the next day.

Ironing was not Wade's thing, but a can of spray starch covered a lot of mistakes and wrinkles. He watched a game for a while and decided that it was boring, then shut it off.

Rikki called at 7:15 and they chatted about the photography book store she found.

Lights out.

It is hard getting used to an alarm that early in the morning, but Wade's bank account said .. get up.

The routine was set and Wade greeted Steven 8-to-4, who pointed out a few things including a box at the side of the doorman's booth that was marked "Wade."

Wade locked the door after Steven slipped out and settled in. He opened the box. On top was a letter from Doc stating this was the first of the collection for the time box and that Wade should make a list on the clipboard included. The contents looked like ordinary household items. Each had a number on it. So Wade poured a cup of coffee and started a list of the contents for the future.

> "What you got there, son?" asked the fireman.
>
> "My stuff. I'm running away from home."
>
> "Oh. Tell your mother?"
>
> "No. She wants me to eat liver. I ain't going back."
>
> "Umm. What you going to do when you grow up? Now that you've run away from home?"
>
> The fireman flipped his cap back on his

head and sat down on the back of the fire truck. The boy did the same.

"I'm gonna be a fireman."

"Well, good. You can stay for dinner. We're having Brussels sprouts, Lima beans served with chicken gizzards. That's the favorite food for firemen." The fireman smacked his lips.

The boy opened his sack and popped open the box of cookies and some comic books. They both read Superman and munched cookies. After the cookies were gone, the boy went home.

The contents of the box listed, Wade opened a travel magazine someone had left on the bench. He flipped through it and put it aside. The chores were routine now and since they were so few, time began to drag. He was amazed how comfortable he seemed at that hour. His body seemed to adapt. He hoped his body would easily adapt back to a normal schedule in the future.

He pulled out his notebook and made a list of some people to call for work and felt good about it. Work begets work.

Mort wandered down about five o'clock, coffee cup in hand and barely greeted Wade. He filled his cup from the pot, offered some to Wade and sat on the bench. The ashtray had been replaced by a potted palm. Mort got up in disgust and with great resolve moved the plant from the front part of the bench facing the door to the other end. It blocked his view. He crossed his legs and sipped his coffee.

"Morning, Mort."

"Morning." But it was the type of morning that rated only a grunt.

"Nice column yesterday."

"Thank you." Mort kept looking out the window.

"Different."

"People will think I have a heart. I've spent my career trying to prove otherwise."

"Mort. It will confuse your readers. Confused people start to think. Once they start to think or look for answers, they ... improve. They are tested by seeking the answer to their questions."

Mort turned toward the booth where Wade sat.

"Wade, we seek all our lives. Money. Love. Respect. Happiness. Sometimes we don't know we had it, until it is gone. We underestimate it. Take it for granted. We receive signals that were misinterpreted. We think they mean something else, or have no burden or weight to what we need. Then in frustration we take drastic action and soon we find we have given up something that is very precious and replaced it with something else. Then we miss that which we had."

"We are tested," Wade said.

"You know what is the greatest test of all? Love. Money comes and goes. Respect is momentary. Happiness is fleeting. But love is tested all the time. But if it is love, it endures. Love above all else. I think that comes from the Bible. What did you do before you came to work here?"

"I was a bartender. Now I'm a doorman."

"What is your future?"

"What I want to do when I grow up?" Wade giggled.

"Yup."

"Well ... I don't know. Right now in my life, that is all I do know. I've had fifty jobs. Traveled some. Been unemployed, and ... now I'm employed. Been to museums, seen films, operas. Read some books. Kissed some pretty girls. Spent some money. And it's been good. It's been bad. Had corporate jobs and plain labor. All I know right now is that, I don't know. Am I clear?"

"Reading your road map of life to see where you been in order to see where you're going."

Wade thought of his dad driving the car as his mother fumbled with an unyielding road map. The more his mother tried to fold it, the more his father got steamed.

"Your diary is merely your checking of the scenery, the countryside as you go slow. You're reconnoitering yourself. Where am I? Who am I? What am I doing? Your diary is a good start."

"My diary?"

"Your notebook. Journal." Mort pointed.

"Oh."

"Life is the coming together of three things." Mort paused and sipped his coffee and continued.

"Life is someone to love, something to do, and a dream. If you loose the first one, you are lost." Mort poured another cup of coffee and started down the staircase to the basement.

"Remember, it's Romeo and Juliet. Not Romeo and Brenda."

Wade watched him go.

The dog walkers did their walks, and the early risers and corporate types were all out the door. Some leaves were blown in and Wade grabbed the broom and dustpan. Henry came in later than usual and took the box of things downstairs. He only nodded and that was that.

Wade put on his cap and straightened his tie as he stretched his legs. The mail came and the cleaners dropped off some hanging garments. The rental agent dropped by with some prospective tenants for the apartments and with a wave of her hand indicated that Wade was the doorman and always on duty.

"The painting to your right, early Matisse, points out his extreme period. Meaning his shortsightedness."

The tour leader pointed, waited, then moved on.

The little boy paused, pulled out his own drawing and taped it under the Matisse and stood back to admire his work. Then he rushed to catch up with the rest of the group.

"Mommy, my picture is in the museum."

"Good, dear."

"Mommy, it is. It is."

"I believe you, honey."

"It is!"

"I know, dear. I can feel it with all my heart."

The boy ate his dinner and wondered.

The agent and her clients went up the elevator.

A gust of wind opened the front door and more leaves blew in. Wade turned and grabbed the broom. Standing in the middle of the leaves was Sheliah.

"Tell me a story." She looked at Wade.

"Tell me a story about the life of a rich king in a faraway land. Tell me a story about people who build monuments to their greatest kings. Of an era when people ate off golden plates and worshipped the sun. I want to be warm and I want to be rich. I want to be remembered as … a solar deity." She picked at the blue nail of her baby finger with the black nail of her thumb.

"You can play the music that you wrote in your book."

She moved out of the leaves and across the hallway and down the stairs, her shawl riding her arms.

Wade swept up the leaves and shook his head.

Noon. Wade looked at the door. Junior was running a little late but no big deal.

The phone rang.

"Lobby." Wade answered. Junior entered and gave Wade a slap on the back. He slipped down the stairs and was back in a flash. No damage done.

"Henry wants to talk to you before you leave," said Junior. He offered Wade his popcorn. Wade pointed to something in the day book and Junior nodded.

"You need something, Henry?" Wade entered the small office carrying the box for the time vault. Henry pulled his feet down from the desk.

"Wade, you happy working here?" Henry stood.

"Umm, sure, Henry. I'm broke and I need to work. I don't like the hours, but a broke man can't complain. A job's a job. You know. I get something better, I would take it. But I would give you fair warning. You've been good to me."

Henry sat back down and picked up the plumber's wrench and started hitting the side of the desk.

"Am I doing okay on the job?"

Henry nodded.

"Anything else? Long night. Coffee didn't kick in like it usually does. I want to go home and get a nap." Wade loosened his tie.

"Mr. Murkoff called, wants you to come up to his office." Henry handed Wade a slip of paper.

"What's he want with me?" Wade looked at the paper.

Henry said nothing. Wade looked at Henry and turned and left. The carpenter's shop was open and Wade went over to the small table that served as desk and dinner table. Doc and Mort were playing cards.

Mort looked happier than a Florida retiree holding a fistful of spades. He was puffing on his cigar, his tam low over his eyes, his glasses perched at the end of his nose. The cards were frayed and the score on the wall, kept at a dollar a point, was barely legible. Umpteen zillion to something. Miss Socket Wrench 1957 hid part of the score.

Mort held his cards with both hands. Doc laid his cards face down. Wade watched for a minute then went over to the wall where the time vault had started to mount up. Wade placed the box to the side and imagined the completed project.

Henry walked into the shop and went over to the card game. He started to talk and then noticed Wade. Henry looked at Doc and Mort. Doc nodded.

"More bricks are coming this afternoon. I got some asbestos covering for the inside," said Henry.

"Two more days." Doc said. Henry looked at Wade and left.

Wade sat down at the card table and Doc started talking.

"Farm life is tough."

"Tell me about it." Mort prompted.

"Fat old man Barnett was the town police chief, as a prank, we placed a carriage up on the old school building. Took it apart and put it back together up on the roof. Couldn't prove it was me or any of the other young 'uns in the town, but my parents decided to send me to the farm to visit my grandparents. Things are tough on the farm."

Mort threw down a couple of cards.

"First day, my grandfather made me do some plowing." Doc slapped down some cards. "You see how hungry you get plowing forty acres behind a mule. Grandpa looked at me and said this or an education. What's it going to be? About that time the mule cut the cheese and I knew the answer."

Mort sounded it out. Wade smirked. Doc's Marlboro hung from his lips and his eyebrows hung low, shielding his eyes from the smoke. He pulled a couple of cards from the discard pile.

"Last time I saw my grandparents was the night before I left for school."

"When was that?" asked Mort.

"September 1927."

Mort pulled a couple of cards from the pile. Wade calculated Doc's age. He looked pretty good.

"My grandmother prepared a big meal. Grandpa opened a big jug of corn. Best liquor I ever tasted. Grandpa got drunk.

Grandma started crying. The more Grandma cried, the more Grandpa drunk."

"Happy to see you go to college," said Wade.

"Grandma was crying because Grandpa had butchered Omar the bull. It was her pet."

Doc wrote a score on the wall.

"I was the first man in the family to get an education. I could read and write. My grandfather wanted to have a celebration. A steak dinner. They sold the rest of the meat to buy me a new suit."

"They must have been very proud." Mort shuffled the cards.

"Yes, they were simple folk. My grandfather tried to make a speech but the corn got to him and he passed out. My grandma crying. Me, sitting there holding my new suit and looking at my steak."

"Omar the bull!" Mort sorted his new cards.

"About three months later, my grandparents died of... broken hearts, I guess." Doc swallowed.

"My grandfather killed my grandmother, then himself. I got the farm, to pay for my schooling. He explained it all in the will. They had had a good life. It was an end of an era."

"Your grandparents loved you very much to make that sacrifice," Mort said. Wade felt a pall come over him.

"Yes. They were farmers."

"Tell me about your schooling, Doc." Mort lifted his

cards and blew smoke at them to hide something. But his eyebrows gave it away.

"I studied dentistry."

"You were a dentist?" Mort put his cards down.

"I never worked as a dentist. It's not something I'm proud of ..."

"You don't have to tell me if you don't want to."

"It's a black mark against my name." Doc looked over to the corner by the chimney and the start of the brick work.

"Let the record show no bruises or contusions to life." Mort waved his hand. Doc smiled.

"School did charity work in the poor neighborhoods. Poor in those days meant poor, not white or colored. Couldn't afford to hate anybody. I set up a little shop. Did odd things, simple stuff. When something major came along, I sent them over to the dentist who was assigned to teach me. We were paid in tokens, chickens, mending, Sunday dinners. Laundry. But never money. Money was a dream!"

"So what happened?" Mort drew two cards.

"Oh ..." Doc took a sip of coffee. "... one day this father came in with his daughter, maybe ten years old. Her gum was infected on the left side." Doc touched the spot on his own jaw.

"She was bad off. Shoulda gone to the hospital. Father started crying, because the dentist wouldn't help poor coloreds. I did what I could. Three days later, I got off the trolley and I saw this crowd coming toward my shop. The father was carrying the girl. The left side of her face was swollen the size of a melon. Eye swollen shut. Awful."

"Gaww ..." Wade raised his eyebrows.

"I put them both in a cab and took them over to the dentist's office, kicked out his patient, made him take care of the girl."

"Did the dentist refuse?" Mort looked over his cards at Doc.

"Nobody refuses when you got a .44 pointed at your head." Doc shrugged.

"She had to go to the hospital. She could have died. Took my savings and paid the hospital bill. I was responsible. I knew then I didn't want to be a dentist. I never wanted to see that look in a father's eyes again. Dropped out of school in 1928. October."

Doc and Mort played a couple of rounds of cards. Wade watched.

"What did you do in 1929?" Mort asked.

"Whisky and women." Doc smiled.

"I fooled around. Traveled out west. Picked apples. Ended up in North Dakota. Worked as a mechanic for a crop dusting outfit. Those days, cars and planes were pretty much the same, so they hired me."

"Teeth to carburetors. I'll remember that." Mort played a card.

"Good, you can be useful." Doc slapped a card on the pile.

"Boss didn't show up for work one day. Big landowner wanted some crops dusted, so I did it. Boss wondered where the extra money in the till came from. I told him and he laughed. Gave me the money for cheering him up. Boss knew it wasn't true 'cause the parachute was in his truck. Four days later the landowner came by and wanted more done, said we did a good job. The boss, Ray, that was his name, couldn't believe that I had gone up in one of those rickety planes without a parachute. Word got out that I was a 'crazy man.' So I left."

"Weren't you scared, Doc?" Wade asked.

"No. Just didn't figure I'd jump out of a plane. Ride it down and take my chances!"

"Pretty brave, for a fool." Mort played his cards and Doc took the game. Wade stood as the two men figured out the points and added to the wall, never to be paid.

"See you later Doc, Mort."

"Wade, here is a poem or something written on the back of this here card. Will you put it in that poetry book of yours. Me and Doc think young guys like you should have a copy of it." Mort pulled out the piece of paper and handed it to Wade.

To Wade

My diddly days are over.

My pilot lights are out.

What used to be my sex appeal
Is now my water spout.
I remember, on its own accord
From my trousers it would spring,
Now I have a full-time job
To find the damn thing.
It used to be embarrassing
The way it would behave,
For every single morning
It would stand and watch me shave.
As my old age approaches
It sure gives me the blues
To see it hang its little head
And watch me tie my shoes.
From Mort and Doc

Wade folded the piece of paper and stuck it in his back pocket.

Junior was at his station in the lobby talking to an six year old boy named Luke. Luke was the product of divorce, and his father lived across the street, and his mother, Pamela, lived in Sixty-Six. Certain days here, some across the street on visitation. Luke was riding his tricycle around the lobby.

"We're going to Colorado for Christmas." Luke kept riding.

"Mommy is staying here and Daddy and his new girl friend are taking me to see the volcanoes." He got off his trike and began wiping off dirt with his handkerchief.

"You gonna ski on these volcanoes?" Junior winked.

"No, I don't think so. Mommy says that Daddy's new girl friend's got a big 'wung' and it won't fit on the chair lift."

Junior looked at Wade and they laughed.

Wade dropped his bag when he got home and took a quick shower. His appointment with Murkoff was not until two, but he decided to walk up to midtown and grab a bite to eat on the way. He put on his gray slacks and blue blazer and striped tie, a white shirt, of course. The collar was a little wrinkled, so Wade gave it a blast of spray starch and ironed it on the kitchen table. He thought of what an extra job might mean, because he owed some money and to eradicate that problem would mean a better way of life. Maybe this was it.

The secretarial warlord with the blue tinted hair squinched her nose like a rabbit and grilled him, because her boss had not informed her of Wade's appointment.

"Young man, are you sure your appointment is for today?"

"Yes."

"Mister Murkoff did not inform me."

"I'll wait."

Wade sat down and pondered the Eleventh Commandment.

"Thou shalt not 'blue' thy hair."

As the secretary thumbed her appointment book, Murkoff strode through the door. Without stopping, he breezed into his office, instructing Wade to follow. Wade squinched his nose in a parting shot to the secretary.

Alvin Murkoff put down his briefcase and stood looking at Wade. He then went to the window and the view. The view was of another executive looking back at Murkoff. Wade giggled, for each man was looking for an answer.

> "Put the bait on the hook for me, Daddy."
>
> "Gotta do it yourself."
>
> The boy put the worm on the hook and threw the line into the water.
>
> "We're gonna catch a whopper, Daddy."
>
> "You betcha, son."
>
> The boy sucked on a reed, and the father lit a cigar and enjoyed the afternoon breeze.

Murkoff turned from the window and offered him a cigar. Wade accepted the cigar but put it in his pocket.

"Wade, I've tried to size you up."

Murkoff sat down. Wade sat.

"A hundred guys in a bar, watching the ball game. A few beers, we're all buddy-buddy. Three women get together, it's two against one immediately. Hell, you know why they all go to the can together? So they don't talk about each other!" Murkoff sucked on his cigar and watched Wade.

No reaction.

"But I'm the guy who buys a round for them all, men and women. You know why? Because people like me." Murkoff picked up his half-glasses and twirled them by the ear piece. His manicured nails caught the glint of the sun reflected off the other temple of commerce across the street.

"Wade, I want you to work for me."

"I already do. Doorman."

"No, Wade. More. Better."

"Doing what?"

"Investments. The future is investments." Murkoff must have thought he had just made a pronouncement equal to the Second Coming.

"Greed propels the human being. Hunger. Sex. There are easy women all over the place. Our society is overfed. That leaves greed. Money. Investments."

Murkoff began a tale of his humble beginnings and how he had built an empire of real estate investments for doctors and lawyers by using the telephone.

"It's easy. Call up these rich professionals and sing them a song about wealth building in real estate and how they can pyramid their money. They make money. You make money. What do you think?"

> "Mommy, there are no cookies in the jar."
>
> "Did you clean your room like I asked?"
>
> The boy shook his head and pouted.
>
> "Nobody puts cookies in your cookie jar except yourself."
>
> The boy padded down the hallway and cleaned his room. Milk and cookies were served at bedtime.

Murkoff waited for an answer.

"I'll certainly think about it."

"Good. That's exactly the answer I expected from you, Wade. Maybe I have sized you up correctly." Murkoff came around from his desk and patted Wade on the back. But just before he opened the door to let Wade out, their faces six inches apart, he said.

"Wade, I've got a sizable investment at Sixty-Six. You let me know if there is any hanky-panky going on. Employees ripping me off. That's a first-rate building, but some of those people I don't trust. You call me. I'll pay well to protect my investment. Here's my home number. Call me if something comes up." Murkoff handed Wade his business card.

Murkoff stepped into the reception area and instructed the secretary to call a car service for Wade. Wade shook him off and walked home. The walk would do him good.

When Wade got to his apartment, the phone was ringing. It was Rikki and Wade told her about the job offer. She seemed excited. Wade told her the same answer that he told Murkoff. Rikki agreed that it was best to think about it.

That was why he liked her. They thought alike. It was not a tug of war on ideas. They both wanted an easy path for their lives. Even his thoughts about her created a gentle hum.

Wade stated that he was going to take a nap and he would talk to her tomorrow. He put Murkoff's card on his desk, undid his tie, dropped his pants to his skivvies and thought he might jog before he went to bed that night. His sleep routine was odd and his eating times off, and this last week he had no opportunity to work up a good sweat. But the phone rang.

It was Jay, the bartender from the Rusty Anchor. They talked for a few minutes and Wade agreed to come over and help Jay with whatever he was doing in the building of his plane, the pterodactyl.

Jay's apartment was on the top floor of a building facing the river about four blocks from the Rusty Anchor. Wade walked by the restaurant, but it was still empty. He thought about the life that had existed within the walls of the restaurant

— happiness, sadness, barroom brawls, and celebrations. And how life converged to that point for events to happen. If the bar had not existed, would those events have occurred?

If the book store where he met Rikki had not existed, would they have ever met? Would their lives have intersected at some other junction? Would his deep feelings for her and the things that he did for her that seemed to fall into place so easily have happened, a clear indication that this was the woman for him? What else could he believe?

And now, after being out of work so long, to have met Henry at the Rusty Anchor and ending up with a job that led to Mort and Doc and Alvin Murkoff .

Now what did Jay want?

Jay opened the door of his apartment and greeted Wade with a sweep of his arm and said, "There is my baby!"

What Wade saw was a loft with windows affording a view of the river and a small cot to one side and a disorganized carpentry shop with sawdust on the floor. There was a lathe, some piles of two by fours, a stack of plywood sheeting, and what looked like ribbing to something.

Jay closed the door. On the back of the door were the designs and blueprints that Jay had shown Wade at the bar months ago.

"Wade, grab a beer from the refrigerator." Jay didn't wait and went to the refrigerator and opened beers for each of them.

"I need your help, buddy. But first, I got to swear you to secrecy."

Wade shrugged.

"This design of mine will be valuable information. Others will want to have it and will pay big to get it. But you, I can trust."

Jay showed Wade around the shop, pulling out this piece of wood, putting it back, another piece there. Wade sipped his beer. The sky had been overcast earlier but now the far side of the river could be seen and Wade's attention was diverted by the view.

"That's where I want to fly to."

"Where?"

"I want to fly across the river and land there." Jay pointed to a tall building on the Jersey side.

"On the roof."

"How're you going to do it?"

Jay's shoulders dropped.

"Wade, my design." His arms swept around the room again.

"My pterodactyl will fly me across the river. I'll land on the roof and I'll fly back. I'm going to prove that the past can come alive again. That today is the future. That my pterodactyl, the past, will live in the future." Jay was near shouting.

"I'm not going to fly with you."

"No, Wade. I need you to help me take this thing to the roof!"

Wade let out a breath of fresh air.

"When are you going to fly this prehistoric chicken?"

Jay gave Wade a look as they carted the bits and pieces out the door and up the steps to the roof.

"Couple of days. I have to assemble it, then test it. A few hops around the roof, ten feet or so. Then I go."

The design was smaller than originally drawn. From wing tip to wing tip it was forty feet. Jay pulled out a tarp and covered all the parts and tied it down.

"I told the landlord that it was an art piece, so as not to attract attention. Nobody will bother me up here." The wind picked up and a breeze flapped the edge of the tarp.

"Good breeze like this will fly me into the future."

"What if you crash?" Wade asked.

"I won't."

Wade looked across the river to the building, the intended landing spot. It looked serene when viewed through an apartment window. But now, as a distant destination across busy streets, buildings, a stretch of murky water, the landing spot, some thirty stories up, looked frightening.

"You got a parachute?"

"No. Too heavy."

"How about a will?"

"No. I got this thing to do. You don't die until you do

your things in life."

Wade sipped his beer and looked back across the river.

"You gonna fly back, right?"

"Yup. Early in the morning."

"Jay, call me when you take off."

"Aren't you going to be here?" Jay made a plantiff sound.

"No. I'd like to. I got to work."

Jay lashed down the flapping tarp and looked across the river.

"This is gonna be great!" Jay shouted and went down the stairs.

Wade walked to the edge of the roof and looked over. A trash dumpster was at street level. He tilted back the last of his beer and aimed the can at the dumpster. It whistled on the way down and went in. Bull's-eye.

Wade wandered back to his apartment and did his chores. Bachelor chores, much shorter than married people chores. A sweep of the broom is okay. Clothes folded once, okay. He picked a book from his library and put it in his bag and pulled his notebook out and made a list of things to do next week. He stapled a couple of food coupons to a page for when he went grocery shopping. Twenty-five cents off something is like picking up a quarter on the street.

He opened a can of soup and put it on the stove. The wind was whipping around the building and the cracks caught some of it and chiseled into the apartment. He was cozy, but winter was letting him know it was still here.

7:15 p.m. He called Rikki and chatted for a moment about Jay and his plane.

"'He's crazy," Rikki said. "Can't you stop him?"

"No. He wants to do it. He is a pilot. Trained. If he wants to fly into the river or to another building or crash, I can't stop him."

"But he's your friend."

"I have a choice. I let him go and he comes back, then I was the one who believed in him. If I try to stop him, he will hate me forever. I have to decide whether I believe in him or I think he's nuts. I think, he's going to be okay."

"But you don't know for sure?"

"No. I'm not a pilot or an engineer. I'm just his friend." Wade stirred the soup.

"Wade, would you let me do that?" she asked.

"No. You're not a pilot."

"I mean would you let me go do something you didn't like."

"Like what?"

"I don't know. Maybe something I thought I had to do, but you didn't like." She paused.

"Rikki, my love for you is in full bloom and growing. It has built over a long period of time. And you are my best friend. I would ask that you not do something, whatever. But I would have to let you do it, if my resistance caused you tremendous grief. But I would pray."

"Do you pray, Wade?"

"Yes."

"Umm."

"I would pray that you come back to me."

"And if I didn't?"

"I would be lost. Alone and scared."

"Would you cry, Wade?"

"Probably ... yes. Do you think that is a sign of weakness?"

"No. It would be a sign that you loved me."

"Yes, I do. So don't go. Simple as that."

"But if I did go, did this thing. And if I did come back ..." she searched.

"You would be stronger and happier. And you would know one thing ... that my love for you is true, unwavering."

"How would I know that?"

"Because love is more like an old sweater that feels comfortable when you put it on. Fills you with warmth and joy, and you wonder why you took it off in the first place."

"Wade, that is so beautiful."

"Rikki, I care for you very deeply."

"Umm. I guess I never asked."

"You never asked because you are happy. Or I read you as happy."

"Read me?"

"Your actions. The tone of your voice. The way you touch me. The way you look at me. Your eyes. Little things."

"But I have trouble reading you, Wade."

"Oh. I thought I was an open book. Especially around you."

"You hide your inner thoughts."

"I value them and the combination is slowly being given to you. I thought by now you could open the safe any time you wanted and find the contents of my heart. Yours for the taking."

"Simple as that?"

"Yes. If I'm sometimes hard to read, just ask."

"Okay."

"So, are you planning on doing something I might not like?" he asked.

"I don't know."

"You seem to know a lot."

She giggled.

"Wade, if I go ... and then come back ... what would be the easiest way for me to come back? If I knew you had been unhappy?"

"The best way would be to walk up to me and smile and ask if I'd like a cup of coffee. Sound familiar?"

She giggled again. Wade always liked to hear her laugh and liked that he could make her laugh.

"You make it sound so easy, Wade."

"It is, when you love someone. All else falls in place."

"Wade, I miss you."

"Rikki, I miss you, too."

They hung up. Wade started the process for bed. When he fell asleep he dreamed.

How Onions Got Their Tears

"You there! Grow!"

The old man patted the earth around the onion, then got up as fast as his knees would let him.

"Who does he think he is?" asked Ruby Red.

"He's the man who owns the garden we grow in," said Boyia, an onion.

"Well, he should be more careful," Ruby Red said gruffly.

"Ruby, we are onions. We need to be patted and hoed and weeded so that we grow big and strong." Boyia was so reassuring. That is why Ruby liked him.

But one day the old man came and pulled up the carrots and celery and some lettuce and then reached over and grabbed the top of Ruby and pulled her out.

"Boyia!" She screamed. "Good-bye."

And Boyia looked up to the sky and asked.

"What happened?" and he wept.

CHAPTER SIX

When Wade awoke to the bedside alarm, he heard a noise that sounded familiar but could not recall. It was the other alarm going off on the table. Both alarms disoriented him. And he grabbed the baseball bat he kept by the bed and stood in the dark ready to do battle.

"Mommy, Mommy, Mommy." The boy screamed from his crib. The mother rushed in and grabbed the boy and hugged him.

"It's all right, baby."

"Mommy, the clowns were going to cook me!"

The mother and the boy turned toward the wall. Three clown faces were framed above the crib.

"The clowns, Mommy. They were going to eat me."

"Bad clowns. Bad. Bad."

Mommy hit the pictures with her hand and put the boy back down in his crib. But

Mommy left the room and the boy could see
the faces of the clowns waiting for Mommy to
leave the room.

Wade recovered his senses and turned off the two alarms by touching the top of the clocks with the bat.

"Bad clowns."

The front door to Sixty-Six was locked, and when Wade pushed the night buzzer, nobody responded. Steven was probably downstairs washing his hands.

Wade walked out to the curb and waited. The night air grabbed his lungs and it felt good. He looked up the side of the building toward the sky. A couple of apartments had their lights on. Mrs. Donaldson, probably watching a late movie. The Irishman on twelve, drinking. But the building looked like a pillar to the sky, only inches from the stars. The next stop on the elevator would be the heavens.

"Sorry, Wade." Steven 8-to-4 opened the door and came out on the street.

"I was looking at the building. Very majestic." Wade leaned back with his hands in his pockets.

"Uxmal," said Steven.

"What?"

"Uxmal. Temple in Mexico where the people came to worship. Serpents carved on the steps that led to heaven."

"Now what is it, a tourist trap?"

"Sure, what else? People got to eat, not die."

Wade laughed for a minute and watched Steven light a cigarette. They stood there for a few minutes, then Steven threw the cigarette into the gutter and went inside. Wade stood at the curb, admiring the sky.

That sound again. He hadn't heard it in a few days, but here it was again.

Steven came out with his overcoat and waved goodbye.

"Steven, you hear something?"

Steven cocked his ear.

"No."

"You don't hear something. Like a train whistle?"

"When I came here and started these hours, I thought I saw pink cats wandering around. But it turned out to be Mrs. Donaldson walking her poodle in a pink robe." Steven left.

But Wade heard the train whistle again. It rose and then fell and rose again, far off in the distance. Then ceased. Wade shook his head and went inside.

The night book had its regular list of chores and another box of stuff from Doc was off to the side. Wade opened it and was amazed that the contents were not those that might impress someone in the future, but used household goods, like a can opener, a cork screw, a deck of cards, a pencil, aspirin tablets, a fork, a plate, a teakettle. The note asked if Wade had anything to donate to the future.

Wade wrote a note in the logbook and then made sure

the door was locked. He made a fresh pot of coffee and kicked off his shoes. He opened the book he had brought from home and started to read *The Time Machine* by H. G. Wells.

Wells must have been a very unhappy man to want to travel back and forth in time. Wasn't life good here? Life is life, no matter where you are.

The coffee was ready and the aroma filled the lobby and made the room cozy. The Christmas lights on the tree added a glow. But the coffee did not taste good. There was an aftertaste. He spit out the first sip and checked the pot.

He smelled the coffee pot and sniffed the coffee beans. He shrugged his shoulders and put the cup to the side and continued to read. After about fifteen minutes his eyes began to tire and he decided to write a short story in his notebook. He pulled the book out of his bag and started to write but his mind began to wander. Finally, he checked the door a second time, went back to the booth and lay his head down on the desk. He had never done this before and felt guilty and started up several times, looking around. But his body had not received its dose of caffeine and finally his head rested on his notebook.

"Wade. Wade."

Wade brushed aside a tickle from his ear and sat straight up. He looked at the door and turned to see Mort sitting on the bench. Mort was in his usual dirty shirt, spotted shoes, tam at the back of his head.

"Have another cup of coffee," Mort said. "Newspapers

come yet?"

Wade got up and went to the door, unlocked it and went outside. At the corner he saw a bundle of papers, brought them in and placed them on the desk. He pulled out Mort's copy and handed it to him.

Mort flipped to his column, made a quick glance, then shut the paper and put it in his lap. Wade opened the paper and read the column.

> Not blue blood. He can break wind from both ends. His hair goes thataway. His teeth are long and crooked. His nose is close to the middle of his face. His shoulders stooped over.
>
> Not blinking. His eyes can see the future.
>
> Not bending. His will is as solid as the granite his name is carved on.
>
> Not affected. By mocking of others. He stands as a model to man. Tested by time. His patience is longer than the summer day. His hands are vises that can crush steel, yet hold babies close to his heart. He speaks truth in an age of false verbosity. He's seen time heal all wounds. Heels wounded by time.
>
> He has looked his Creator in the eye and shook His hand. He has been asked to travel a road that has no return.

What better man to be chosen than one who believes.

An honor all men wish. But only good soldiers travel this path.

We will meet in another realm.

Let the trumpets blare.

Let the crowds cheer.

There stands a man among men.

Good-bye my sweet and gentle friend.

Wade folded the paper and put it back in the pile. He looked at Mort who sat on the bench sipping his coffee.

"I'm sorry, Mort. A good friend died?"

Mort did not say anything to Wade but looked out the window and finished his coffee. He then rose and went up the elevator.

The routine of the dog walkers started. Wade did not have the heart to greet each and every one. He waved, he nodded. Henry scooted in but did not acknowledge Wade.

The other employees nodded when they came in, and a couple put Christmas presents under the tree. There had been mention of a Christmas party on the Eve, but most had opted out due to family. Wade had planned to take the bus up to see his parents for a couple of days. He wanted to see them, but he also needed the work. His father would understand and eventually so would his mother.

The mail arrived and parcels from the delivery service. Doc came in and asked for the box that Wade had catalogued. “Drop downstairs, will you, Wade, after your shift. I need to talk to you about the ... you-know-what.”

Wade nodded.

The morning dragged on. The coffee had an acid taste to it, so Wade had no juice in his batteries. He thought of Doc’s pot of coffee in the carpentry shop and set his mind on a nice cup at noon.

The sun took the chill out of the air. It was odd that the Christmas season wasn’t as cold and snowy, he remembered as a boy. Some afternoons could be tolerated with a sweater or light jacket. Gone were the deep snow banks he had played in as a youngster. He couldn’t even remember the last winter, that had been truly cold with deep snow.

Sheliah entered the first set of doors, waited until the doors closed behind her, then shut her eyes, inhaled the vestibule air and screamed. She spread her arms, lifting her cape. She composed herself and passed through the second set of doors, then turned and looked back outside.

“It will end when you see two moons.”

She looked at Wade and he stared right back. She did not waiver. She did not blink. She turned and descended the employee staircase.

Wade went outside and looked up and down the street.

He looked up in the sky.

No moon.

But he did see Jimmy Grease across the street walking toward the corner. His hands were in his pockets and his clothing looked disheveled. He looked like the old Jimmy, the greasy one, not the clean Jimmy handling out Bibles with Queenie.

"Jimmy."

Jimmy started to walk faster toward the curb. He stopped and picked up some empty beer cans from the garbage and threw them at Wade.

"You piece of manure," Jimmy said. Wade dodged the cans and watched him walk away.

"Who is that?" Wade turned and saw Junior.

"Just an old friend."

"Ex-friend is more like it."

Junior was in a jovial mood and offered Wade some popcorn as he related the fun from the day before. It seems that the tenants wanted to erect a Dutch windmill in the garden at the corner of the block. It was a small plot belonging to the building. A meeting was held in the lobby the night before.

"It got pretty boisterous," recounted Junior.

"The Greens wanted a windmill with anti-littering slogans on the vanes. The Sports wanted a vane that said 'Go Yankees.'

The Politicals wanted vanes promoting the impeachment of somebody. Finally, the action group decided to table the whole windmill idea because someone speculated that the spinning vanes would read as 'Go pick your nose'!"

When Wade and Junior entered the lobby, the phone was blinking. It was Henry asking if Junior had arrived. Junior went downstairs and reappeared ready to work.

Wade checked in with Henry and passed by the carpentry shop. Doc was bent over by the cubicle that he was building. The bricks were now knee high in front and complete all around to the top. An opening from knee height to head was all that was left to be filled in. The cubicle was crammed with stuff, clothing, books, all neatly stacked. A small space in front contained the chair from the desk. A thermometer sat on the chair and Doc was checking the temperature.

"Wade, can you lay bricks?"

"Some. But I'm not a mason."

They practiced on a few. Doc pointed out how to handle the trowel and make a neat groove in the mortar.

"That's very good, Wade. I'd like for you to finish this job." Doc circled his hand to indicate the gaping hole.

"Now?"

"No. When the time comes. I would be honored to have you do it."

"Okay, Doc."

"I'm too old to finish this and a guy like you would do the trick. Can I rely on you?"

"Doc, no problem."

"Good. You'll be my watchdog at the gate. Dogs that

bark aren't as much of a puzzle as those that keep their yaps shut."

Doc took his flashlight and looked inside the time vault. Wade put the trowel away as Henry and Mort entered the shop. Henry closed the door behind him and Mort sat at the card table.

"Come on over here, Wade." Doc sat in his chair and looked at Henry and Mort.

"Veracity. Propriety. Honor," said Mort looking at Wade. Wade nodded. Henry was looking at Doc.

"Wade. I'm dying," Doc said.

Wade did not blink or move.

"Do you believe in your dreams, Wade? I do. I have believed in my dreams since I was your age. I believed then, now, and believe in the future. I believe." Doc stopped talking for a moment and looked at the others.

"I am old. The doctors have told me I will be around forever. But what do doctors know?"

Mort snickered.

"I'm going to be eaten by a turtle." Doc sipped his coffee.

"Does that surprise you that I say I'm dying and I'm going to be eaten by a turtle?"

"No, Doc. If you believe that."

"You think I'm crazy?"

"No. Your dreams are messages. But you might be

reading them wrong."

"Yes, that's right. But I've lived a long time and I believe in my dreams." Doc looked at the others.

"Mort?" Wade asked.

"He believes." Mort pointed to Doc.

"Henry?" Wade turned to Henry.

Henry shrugged his shoulders and then nodded.

"Very appropriate to be eaten by a turtle since it was the turtle that carried the sun across the sky. The ancients ..."

Mort sucked on his cigar and looked over to the chimney and the time vault. Wade turned where he stood and put two and two together.

Doc nodded.

Wade closed his eyes.

"I want to be with my things for eternity. Some carpenter or a plumber will knock down that wall and I will be there to greet them."

"Scare the jeebers out of them!" Mort said.

"Yes. But I will have returned to where I worked and enjoyed some fine hours. Yes. I'll be gone, but my return will give those who find me, meaning to their lives. They will meet someone like them who toiled and sweated. Not a king who was pampered but a working guy."

Doc stood up and put his hand on Wade's shoulder.

"Wade, I want you to finish the job of bricking up the wall when I'm gone." Doc looked at Wade.

"Doc, I'll do whatever you ask. But you will live a long time. Someday, you may pass away, and I will put you in there and seal you up, if that's what you want. Life is too short to think of negative things. Why don't you think about the next card game with Mort or your next project in one of the apartments?"

"Because the dream of the turtle is very clear. Soon." Doc blinked.

"Okay. What do we tell the authorities?" Wade asked.

Nobody moved or said anything. "Ooo-kay. Doc, I've been here a short time and now you've trusted me with a very important project for you. I ... I won't let you down."

Wade shook Doc's hand and looked at each of the others. He climbed the stairs to the lobby and left without saying a word to Junior.

The thought of burying Doc in the wall didn't bother Wade as much as the thought that Doc was looking death in the face. How does one justify such a moment? What do you do before you depart on the last journey? Sex? A ball game? Go to the beach? Look at a sunset? Say good-bye to someone? Say something to your children? Your parents?

What do you say to the ones you love? A glass of wine together. To laugh. To watch their smiles.

Wade stopped in at the deli on the way home and grabbed a cup of soup. As he was paying, the person behind him reached over to grab a napkin from a pile by the cash register and spilled Wade's soup on the counter and onto Wade's slacks. Wade turned to see the culprit.

"Queenie!" Wade shouted in exasperation. She was blotting her lipstick.

"I'm sorry." She cackled that Queen of Hearts laugh.

"You knocked over my drinks at the bar and now my soup. You are haunting me!" Wade wiped the soup from his red slacks and looked at the white spots on his shoes from the clam chowder. Queenie offered to pay for more soup and she did.

"I saw Jimmy this morning."

"He ain't got a dime to his name. You told me he had money."

"I lied. He was down and out. He needed someone to help him in life. You cleaned him up. You made him love you and he loved you, in his own way. Fixed your car? Went to your prayer meetings? Took you to the movies? Handy man stuff around the apartment? He made your life better? Those other guys in the past ... they didn't commit to you because you wanted something." Wade rubbed his thumb and fingers together.

"Jimmy adored you. And that's what you need. He'll work. He'll put food on the table. Give you good babies. The two of you will get all the money you need." Wade picked up his soup.

Queenie bit her lip and lowered her eyes.

"Look. I want you happy. You and I have been around the track. The scar goes a little deeper as we get older. We remember the pain. You lose his love and all that you created and you will have a void. Right about here." Wade pointed to her heart.

"I know," she mumbled.

"Go see him. I know he is unhappy." Wade sipped his soup.

"You talked to him?"

"No. Women never think men have feelings."

"It's been a couple of weeks."

"Time has nothing to do with it. It's what you have learned about being apart." Wade put his hand on her shoulder.

She took a napkin with the lipstick and rubbed a tear and left a trail of lipstick and mascara. "He was kinda funny."

"Love is so easy to repair. Just talk. Get a good night sleep. Go see him tomorrow. Don't be a chicken and call him on the phone. Get him a little something nice."

"We like chocolate chip ice cream." She lowered her sunglasses to her eyes and looked at Wade. A tear pooled in one eye and dropped below the glasses.

Wade put his arm around her shoulder. She lowered her head and left.

Then Wade sneezed.

"If you sneeze, whatever you say after that, is the truth."

A voice came from behind him followed by the sound

of a finger cymbal. It was Sheliah as she approached the deli counter. Her shawl covered her work clothes and her glasses were fogged over and rosy. Wade grabbed his soup and went out the door. The fresh air caught him and he sneezed again.

"I love you Rikki." Wade looked back through the door of the deli and Sheliah looked at him. He toasted his soup to her and walked away.

"Mommy, I hate spelling."

The boy struggled with his homework at the dinner table.

"If you can't spell, you can't write my name."

Mommy dried the dishes.

"I can spell your name. M …O … M."

Mommy laughed.

"Who made up all these stupid words?"

The boy erased.

"People who know." She put the plate up on the shelf.

"Know what?"

"People who know, what's what."

"Well, I know I hate spelling."

"People know other things. You have to believe them."

"Why?"

"They learned other things. But you have to learn how to spell."

Mommy pointed to his work and the boy struggled with ... P.Y.R.A.M.I.D.

"Wade, youse do me a favor?" It was Lucy, the landlady knocking at his apartment door. He looked down at the elderly lady, as she mopped around his door. Her grown children offered a house in the country, but "my Joseph lives here." Wade put on his shoes and went with Lucy to her apartment in the front building.

"Up there." She pointed to the box on the top shelf of the closet. Wade grabbed the kitchen chair. It had a ribbon around it and the corners were frayed. It was the size of a hat box, the top was a flower print and the sides were white. She untied the ribbon.

"This is my Joseph's picture, at the store we ran across the street." Lucy handled the pictures carefully and talked about each one. Letters that were still in the envelopes were reopened, and she would read a line or two then fold them back up. Wade sipped the homemade wine and she "saluted" every time they drank.

Her Joseph was a dark complexioned man that stood head and shoulders above Lucy. His hair was black and wavy and his clothes came from two generations ago. The pictures were yellowing and had white scalloped edges. But even though her eyes were blurry, she saw a clear vision of the man she loved, married, bore children with and buried.

"This the whole family." She pointed to the four children, age five through twelve. But Wade now knew they were in their fifties. She ran her hands over the picture and put it back in the box. Wade wrapped the box with the ribbon.

"Leave the box here. I look later. Do me a favor. Come back tomorrow. Put up on shelf. Okay?"

She gave Wade an extra cookie and Wade made sure she locked her door when he left.

7:15 p.m.

The phone rang and Wade jumped out of bed. He looked at the clock. How could he have overslept his nap? He shook his head. It's wasn't the alarm that was ringing. It was the phone.

He pulled himself out of the fog and accepted Rikki's invitation to dinner.

He stopped at the wine shop for a nice bottle of red wine and went by the florist for the last single rose.

"I thought we'd have dinner over the coffee table." She kissed him for the flower and the wine and took his coat. She looked like spring when she opened the door. Her hair was up and her eyes had that dewy look.

The coffee table had placemats and plates and in the center was a short, squatty blue candle. She returned from the kitchen with the flower in a clear glass vase and handed him the corkscrew for the wine. By now, Frisco Fred had sniffed his shoes and clawed up the couch to Rikki. Wade sat opposite her.

“To us, Merry Christmas.” Wade offered a toast and Rikki lit the blue candle.

“This candle ... gives off a warm glow. Warmer than the truth.” She played with the flame with the match stick. Rikki let out a sigh.

“Rikki ... I ... Doc, the carpenter at the building wants to be put in to the time vault when he dies.”

She shook her head and asked why.

“He wants to be among his things. He believes he will come back someday.”

“Well, we live in our apartments amongst our things and when we die we are put in the ground in a dress or suit we never wear. Interesting. Do you think he’s going to die soon?”

She played with the kitten.

“No, but he thinks he is. Sad. I think he should look forward to tomorrow.”

“His tomorrow is ... in the future.” She sipped her wine.

Wade looked around the apartment and all that she had done to decorate, a wreath with blue lights. A Christmas tree,on the dining room table with blue flocking. On a book shelf was a Nativity scene, she made with clay. On the end table was a framed photograph of them on a street corner, waving to the camera.

“Here. Merry Christmas.” She thrust forward a small

wrapped gift. He could tell it was a book.

"Thank you. Can I open it?"

"No. Christmas morning. Thank you for my gift." She dangled her snowflake "booby knocker" and the kitten swiped at it.

"When are you leaving to see your parents?" Wade flipped the present from side to side.

"Wade. I'm leaving on the train at midnight." She put her glass down.

"Tonight? Now? In a couple of hours?"

"Yes. I'm staying longer than I planned." Rikki sat up.

"What do you mean? Staying longer than planned? Your parents all right?"

"Yes. Wade … I'm going to stay there for awhile. I don't know how long."

"What are you talking about Rikki? Don't know how long?"

"I just feel ... that I should stay with my parents for awhile ... to think things out." Rikki wiped a tear from her eye.

He looked at her for a minute.

"Think things out? About us? Rikki?" Wade saw the tear form and handed her his pocket square from his jacket.

"Wade ... I ... I ..." Tears flowed from her eyes and she shook uncontrollably. Wade started to get up to sit beside her.

"No ... stay over there." Wade sat back down. Rikki got control of herself.

"I've been thinking about this for a couple of months."

"Couple of months?" Wade shook with fear.

"Yes."

"But you haven't shown any …."

"I know." She sniffed.

"Rikki what's wrong? Please tell me."

She shook her head.

"Rikki .. please ... tell me ..." Wade begged.

"I ... just ... feel … that I should go away for awhile."

"When are you coming back?"

Her body shook with sobs.

"Rikki you got to come back … your home. Your life. Us. Here. Rikki."

Rikki kept her head lowered and tried to gain her composure. Wade sat for a couple of minutes. The kitten played with the snowflake pillow.

"Rikki. I don't know what to say, 'cause you won't tell me anything. Look at me please."

She raised her head and looked at Wade. He held out his hand and she extended hers.

"Rikki do you have love in your heart for me?"

She nodded.

"Tell me when you are going to return?"

She withdrew her hand and lowered her head and cried again..

"What about your apartment?"

"It's been taken care of." Rikki looked up. Tears were coming down both cheeks.

"Please don't cry Rikki." Wade couldn't help himself. He wiped his eyes on his sleeve. They both cried for a minute.

"Will I see you again, Rikki?"

"Yes. Someday. I need time."

"Will we laugh about all this?" Wade asked.

"When I figure this all out."

"Rikki. Talk to me …"

Rikki shook her head and cried again. Deep sobs.

"Rikki, I'll do anything for you, so that you don't cry. Even leave." Wade stood up and Rikki stood too. He went to the closet and got his coat. They stood face to face at the door as she helped with his coat. He leaned over and kissed her and she sighed. His kiss lingered and she moved closer to him. He wanted to put his arms around her and his heart beat faster. A tear flowed down her cheek and Wade felt it on his lips. He pulled back and kissed the next tear.

"Rikki. I love you."

Wade walked out the door and down the stairs. He put his hands in his pockets and walked home. He climbed the stairs to his apartment and opened the door. He took off his coat and jacket. He kicked off his shoes and set the alarms. He laid down on the bed and turned his head to the blue pillow that Rikki had given him and stitched a saying on the fabric.

"Sweet dreams until we meet again." He cried.

CHAPTER SEVEN

Wade did not sleep. His eyes crusted over with crying crystals and his lashes stuck together. His heart was pounding like a locomotive. It felt as if not enough blood was getting to his heart. He had a void in his heart and he sucked in air to compensate. His body was soaking wet and his nose was blocked with mucus. He swung his legs over the bed and looked at the clock across the room. His legs were bloated with blood so he wiggled his toes, flexed his knees and stood to answer the buzzer of the alarm clock. He was standing, not there in the center of his apartment, or anywhere, his mind was in Rikki's apartment listening to the last words she said that made no sense.

Wade sat at his desk and shaved his stubble. His answer machine light blinked. He tapped the replay button. It was Rikki's voice and she was calling from the train station.

"Wade, I miss you."

She said as she muffled her tears and hung up the phone. Wade dropped the shaver and slumped in his chair.

It took a couple of minutes for him to recover and then he reached into his coat pocket that was draped over his chair and found his Christmas present. Like a child he ripped into it he ripped into it and it was a small book.

The inscription page read:

The Book of Wade
by
Rikki
You made my dreams come true.

It was a small book that could easily fit into his hand. He flipped through the book. Each of the two hundred pages contained a saying or phrase.

page 28
Likes chocolate shakes.
page 183
Wade never argues.
page 39
Looks the best in a suit.
page 68
Wade can be very woolly.
page 59
Says something romantic at odd times.
page 35
Can be very forgiving.
page 17
Wade is a clown.

page 47
His smile is huge.
page 94
Takes in stray cats.
page 62
I can talk to Wade about anything. Anything.
page 48
He doesn't think I' m a fool.
page 54
Wade thinks I'm beautiful.

He flipped to the last page.

Wade — I love you.

Wade closed the book and placed it on his desk. He stared at the book and with a sweep of his arms he cleared his desk of all it's contents, except the book and laid his head down on it.

5:00 a.m.

He sat at the doorman's booth and did not move. His hat was cocked back on his head and he stared out onto the street. He could see the glow of the Christmas tree lights on the glass doors. The weather couldn't decide if it would rain or snow, but the wind knew what to do.

Mort wandered down to the lobby with cup in hand and did not say a word. He looked at Wade, offered the coffee pot to Wade's cup but he did not move. Mort shrugged and went and sat down on the bench. The potted plant had been moved back in front of the bench so Mort simply moved the bench.

"Men have two problems in life. Money and women. Now, I can live without a woman a lot longer than I can without money, but it ain't a good life. Is it Wade?"

"No, it's not a good life."

"Women, on the other hand, have to worry about men, money, their hair, and their shoes. They get awfully confused and they end up confusing us. Don't they Wade?" Mort sipped his coffee.

"Yes. She's gone, Mort." Wade lowered his head and lifted his palms to his eyes. "How did you know?" Wade tried to control himself.

"I've been there. I could see it in your eyes. Pain that takes the light out of your eyes, leaves a scar in your heart. It takes a long time to heal."

"What about my Rikki? Will she come back?" Wade turned on the stool.

"A young girl's heart is a finicky thing. Logic does not prevail. It rides on whims and can turn on a dime. Any direction. I don't know … if she cries enough ... realizes what she misses. She'll come back. Everything comes back ... eventually." Mort sipped his coffee.

"I don't know what I did wrong, Mort?" A tear rolled down Wade's cheek, Wade lifted his arms to beg.

"As long as you were honest, and told her, you needed her. What more could you do? Give her some time."

"That's what she said." Wade perked up.

"Women have to make big decisions in life and they all think they have to be made ... now! By themselves. You helped her in the past?"

Wade nodded.

"You will help her in the future. Give her what she needs now. Time."

Wade turned on his stool and looked out the door as the newspaper truck dropped off the bundle. Wade unlocked the door and brought in the bundle. He gave one paper to Mort and took one himself.

"Wade, I'm expecting a package again would you put it aside for me." With that Mort took his paper and went up the elevator.

Wade nodded and folded his paper to Mort's column. He got set to read when the phone rang.

"Lobby."

It was Jay stating that he was doing his final countdown for the past to come into the future. His pterodactyl would fly at dawn. The final bolts had been tightened and the short hops that he took around the roof made him confident that today was the day.

"Good luck ... Jay ... it will work." Wade hung up the phone.

Wade sat at the doorman's booth and rested his head on his hands. Tears dropped into his coffee cup.

9:00 a.m.

"Morning Wade." Doc came in and patted Wade on the shoulder.

"Young man like you, doesn't like to think about death, but when your time comes ... you will look at it as if it's an adventure ... to answer the last great question."

"Doc, I wish you a lot of great adventures and hope that I never have to do as you ask." Wade pointed to the floor in the direction of the carpentry shop and Doc's time vault. Wade reached into his bag and pulled out some menus from his collection of restaurants that he worked in over the years. The Rusty Anchor was on top.

"Hundred years from now, they will still go out to eat. Maybe they would like to see what we enjoyed in our day. Plus here is a cigar for your trip." Wade put the cigar into Doc's breast pocket.

"Thank you Wade." Doc patted his pocket and Wade watched him go down the stairs.

"Wade." Wade turned to see Murkoff standing behind him. They shook hands.

"I haven't heard from you. Friends, aren't we friends?" Murkoff's grip tightened to send a message but Wade returned in kind and Murkoff pulled out of the grip. He wrung his hand to put some feeling back in the hand, looked at Wade then turned and went up the elevator.

Wade picked up the lobby phone and called down to Henry and told him Murkoff was up in the rental office. He sipped his coffee but it was cold and spit it out. He took his cup outside and threw the remains into the gutter. When he turned around Sheliah was standing behind him.

Wade started.

"Good morning, Sheliah."

She looked at Wade and down at the coffee now freezing in the gutter. Sheliah lifted her hand and pointed to the middle of the street and sneezed. Wade looked at the spot and up and down the empty street. Sheliah daintily rubbed her nose and left to go into the building. Wade made another check of the spot and the street and went into the building.

10:00 a.m.

The delivery men all came and went. The secretary called down looking for Murkoff and Henry called twice, same question. The package for Mort came. Wade put it aside.

But Wade was not there. He was searching for Rikki in his heart. The prospect of Christmas seemed a dismal thought. Winter would be cold and nasty. His apartment would be an empty shell, walks in the street would be torture and every snowflake would be a reminder of her.

A void had been created. A living death.

"Come back Rikki, come back please, come back Rikki." Wade hung his head and stood looking out the door.

11:30 a.m.

Mort came down to the lobby and asked about his package and sat down on the bench. Wade gave it to him but they did not speak.

"Would you keep an eye on Luke for me?" asked Pamela as she washed away some breakfast mess from his face and told Luke to play in the lobby. Pamela went up stairs to get something.

"We're going shopping. I need some bolts." Luke unbuttoned his coat and put it on the bench next to Mort.

"Bolts for what?" Mort asked.

"My bike. My dad got me some mud flaps and things." Luke climbed on his trike and rode toward the front door.

"Wow! Look at that! He needs mud flaps for sure," Luke said.

Both Wade and Mort looked out the door and saw a dirty mini-camper parked at the curb.

Wade went out to the curb to greet Fred McIntosh as he climbed out of the camper.

"Good trip Mister McIntosh?" Wade held the door.

"Great trip, but we encountered some nasty roads up north. Look at this dirt. Hey, call me Fred, remember? Wade, do something for me?"

"Ask ... Fred."

"Take these things in and buzz down to Henry to see if he's in his office. I need him to look at the fan belt it seems to be making some sort of whacka-whacka sound." Wade grabbed a load of things and placed them in the lobby.

"Office" But it was Doc's voice. Henry was around and Doc explained he would pass along Fred's request.

Wade continued to help Fred unload the camper and Mort talked to Fred about the trip. Luke rode his bike out to the curb and back with each load of the rolling cart that Wade filled. The last load was placed on the elevator and Fred went up.

"Wade, what seems to be the problem?" It was Doc as he climbed the stairs to the lobby and carried his tool box. "Maybe I can help old Fred and his truck."

"Need any help there, Doc?" Mort asked as Doc passed through the doors.

"Yup. Stay out of the way. Fella like you wouldn't know what a left-handed monkey wrench was." Doc winked at Wade and went out to the camper.

"I know what a wrench is!" Luke piped up as he rode his trike in circles.

The elevator dinged its arrival to the lobby and out stepped Mrs. Donaldson. Both Mort and Wade cringed.

"Wade!" She shrieked from the elevator. She held the leash of her pink poodle. She had a rotund figure and tinted hair.

"Yes Mrs. Donaldson," said Wade. Mort tried to look

invisible.

She harumphed at Mort and the dog snapped at his heels but Mort blew smoke at them both.

"Have you seen Doc?"

Wade pointed outside to the camper. Where Doc had popped the hood and was looking in his tool box. Both Mrs. Donaldson and the poodle pranced outside.

"She is an old witch." Luke rode around on his bike.

All three men watched as Doc bent over the radiator, sticking his head into the engine cavity and started working on the truck as Mrs. Donaldson stood talking to Doc.

"My daddy can fix cars. He put these streamers on my handle bars and he's gonna help me put on these others." With that Luke got off his bike and went over to his coat on the bench and pulled out two white reflectors about three inches across. He held them in each hand.

"We could tape them until you get some bolts, Luke." Wade pulled some tape from his booth and attached each reflector to a handlebar. Luke got off and admired them.

"Moons. They look like moons. I got two moons on my bike." Luke pulled out his handkerchief and wiped the reflectors.

Wade froze and Mort stood up. They both looked out the door to the camper. They saw the full figure of Mrs. Donaldson blocking their view as she passed into the building. She mumbled something about the price of paint and a television show at noon and how Doc didn't hear a word she said.

Wade went outside and slowly approached the camper. Doc was leaning over the front into the engine. Tools protruded from his back pocket.

"What you working on, Doc?" Wade came around to the passenger side of the camper and slowly approached the vehicle.

Doc's tongue was hanging out. Wade stopped and jumped backwards. He looked again. Doc's eyes were popping out and his face was flush with blood. His arms were hanging straight down into the engine well. His glasses were askew. Wade touched him on the shoulder and gave a nudge.

"Doc?"

No answer.

"Wade quickly." Mort was now standing beside the camper.

Wade picked up Doc's limp body and cradled him in his arms. Mort grabbed the tool box and closed the hood. Both Wade and Mort noticed the inscription painted on the hood.

"*Fred's Turtle.*"

Walking swiftly into the lobby and past Luke, Wade carried the very light now deceased Doc down the stairs to the basement.

"Doc is not feeling well, Luke." Mort said.

Traveling past the office and into the carpentry shop,

Wade called out to Henry and he gently placed Doc on the card table in front of a startled Sheliah who had her hands out as if receiving a gift.

"Doc is dead," Wade said.

"I know. My grandfather was eaten by a turtle." She patted Doc's forehead and straightened the wisps of white hair.

Henry entered the shop and closed the door behind him. He touched Doc's neck feeling for a pulse. Then sat down and lowered his head. Sheliah closed her eyes and began to chant.

"Om bah ... Sim bah Wat. Om bah ... Sim bah Wat ."

"Wade put Doc in the vault and let him begin his journey." Mort touched Wade on the arm.

Wade looked to Henry who nodded. Wade placed his arms under Doc and carried him to the vault. Henry removed the thermometer from the chair. Wade adjusted Doc in a sitting position. Mort reached in and placed Doc's coffee cup in his hand. They all stood back and looked at Doc sitting so serenely, ready to go into the future.

"Good-bye, Doc," Wade said. Sheliah waved her hand and kept chanting.

Henry picked up the trowel and handed it to Wade. He took it from him and Henry handed him the first brick. As the final brick was laid in place, Mort unpacked his box that came in the mail.

It was a bronze name plate, inscribed, "D.O.C."

Mort stepped forward and helped Wade place it in the

brick chest high. Wade dropped the trowel and cleaned up the remaining bricks.

"We'll do that Wade. Go on back to the door." Henry swept up some cement mix as Mort stood looking at the name plate and time vault.

"Doc was sick, he's resting down stairs, Luke." Wade spoke to both Luke and Pamela, Luke's mother. Luke was wide eyed, but Pamela grabbed Luke's hand and left the building.

"Fred, Doc fixed your truck." Wade wiped his hands clear of grease as he met Fred coming off the elevator.

"Good. This old 'Turtle' has been a life saver since I retired. No motels for me. Take my home with me. What do I owe Doc?" Fred stopped at the doorman's booth.

"Doc said ... on the house." Wade's voice trailed.

"Doc. Good man. I'll catch him next week." Fred left and climbed into his camper to go park it.

Wade sat down at the booth and lowered his head.

"Look out here comes Murkoff." It was Junior who saw Murkoff get off the elevator. Junior went to the basement.

"Wade, you're a good man to have at the door." Murkoff whizzed by the booth to his limousine.

Junior came back up stairs and he asked Wade if he was okay.

"Yes, I just need a little time off." Wade grabbed his bag and left the building.

Crossing the street he looked down towards Rikki's street and he waved.

In the park, he sat on the bench, the sun felt good on his face, but it was too cold to be warmed by it.

A shadow crossed his face and Wade looked up. In the sun he could see an outline of a prehistoric bird in flight. Lazily, it hung in the sky. Others looked up wondering what it was. It was Jay and the past coming back to the future. Wade smiled and reached over to touch a dried yellow rose preserved in ice until spring.

About the Author

Douglas Gowland is a military brat. He graduated from the University of Texas - El Paso. He lived in Dallas. He catches for his softball team and lives in Greenwich Village, NYC.

VICKI LUVS BOOKS

For further information or to order another copy of this book, please visit the Vicki Luvs web site at www.vickiluvs.com. While you're there, check out the cookies, music and other goodies.

You may write the author or receive more information about Vicki Luvs Books at the following address:

Vicki Luvs
P. O. Box 70091
Houston, Texas 77270

Or you may call toll free at 866-203-5903.